"What kind of welcome is this?" she asked

Rafe shrugged. "I take it you weren't expecting a red carpet and bouquet of roses."

"Red carpet and roses? What are you saying? Why are you so sarcastic? I was so happy to see you. Aren't you happy to see me?"

Something flickered in the dark eyes that swept her face, lingering for just a moment on trembling lips that had once been crushed beneath his. It had been an embrace a desperately unhappy girl had relived over and over again in those first lonely months in America.

"What do you want me to say, Teri?"

"Forget it, Rafe." Her voice was hard now, though there was a glimmer of tears in her eyes as she turned away. "I'd hate you to say anything you didn't want to."

Rosemary Carter began writing short stories that, for a long time, brought only rejections. The turnabout came at the end of her first pregnancy. "It's a memory I cherish," she says, "for the baby was born the day after the acceptance." She lives a few hours away from the Canadian Rockies, and she and her husband love exploring the beautiful mountain trails. But enchantment with her previous home has never waned, and that is why she sets most of her books in the South African bushveld.

Books by Rosemary Carter

Don't miss any of our special offers. Write to us at the following address for information on our newest releases.

Harlequin Reader Service
901 Fuhrmann Blvd., P.O. Box 1397, Buffalo, NY 14240
Canadian address: P.O. Box 603,
Fort Erie, Ont. L2A 5X3

Partners in Passion

Rosemary Carter

Harlequin Books

TORONTO • NEW YORK • LONDON
AMSTERDAM • PARIS • SYDNEY • HAMBURG
STOCKHOLM • ATHENS • TOKYO • MILAN

Original hardcover edition published in 1989
by Mills & Boon Limited

ISBN 0-373-03050-9

Harlequin Romance first edition May 1990

CHAPTER ONE

'MOM! Philip!'

Teri Masters was shaking with excitement as she looked up from the newspaper. Emeralds, thought her stepfather, Philip Willis, not for the first time, as he took in green eyes that sparkled like polished jewels.

'You'll never guess! I've won some money!'

'That's wonderful!' Mary Willis looked up, startled. 'How do you know? How much? How did you win it?'

'Easy, honey.' Philip, ever the steady one in the family, looked with some concern from his wife to his stepdaughter. 'Teri, I'm as curious as your mother. What's this all about?'

'It's here in the paper. The winning numbers. Oh, my goodness, I don't believe it! I've never won a thing in my life.'

Philip peered over Teri's shoulder at the printed lottery results. 'You're sure these are your numbers? Where's your ticket?'

'In my wallet in my bedroom, but I know I've won without even looking. I've played the same numbers all year. Our birthdays. The day you were married. My age. And number thirty-one because California was the thirty-first state of America.'

'And they've all come up?' Her mother was awed.

'Not all. Just five of them.'

'Which,' said Philip, studying the paper, 'may net you winnings of around six thousand dollars.'

Teri pushed excited hands through her shining strawberry-blonde curls. 'Not the fortune I'd have won if *all* my numbers had come up. Still . . .'

'A tidy little sum, all the same,' Philip agreed, laughing.

'Calling for champagne?' suggested Mary.

To which her husband of one year said, 'Just as well I've been keeping that one unopened bottle since New Year's Eve. I must have sensed we'd be needing it for just such an occasion.'

While Philip fetched glasses and champagne, Teri went to find her lottery ticket. And yes, it was as she had expected, the ticket was valid, and she had five of the winning numbers.

There was a plop as Philip opened the bottle and the cork shot across the room. From Mary and Philip were cries of 'Congratulations'. From Teri there was only an overcome, 'Wow!'

They drank several toasts. To the new wealthy one in the family. To the happy combination of birthdays and an anniversary and California's particular situation in the Union. To another win, and 'you just make sure it's a million next time'.

At length, Mary asked, 'What will you do with so much money, Teri?'

'Golly, I don't know.'

'You won't splurge it, will you, darling?'

'Yes! No. Maybe . . .'

'It would make a very nice down-payment on that car you've been wanting for so long.' Philip was smiling.

'That's true,' Teri said thoughtfully.

'More than a deposit. It would go almost all the way to paying for it.'

'I guess that's so.'

'But there's something else you'd rather do.' Mary, who knew her daughter so well, recognised the look that had appeared in the lovely wide green eyes.

'It's just a thought. And maybe it's quite crazy...'

'Teri?' There was the faintest tinge of apprehension in Mary's tone.

The look Teri shot her mother was a pleading one. 'I think I'd like to go to Africa.'

'Africa?' Philip was astounded. His wife just looked stunned.

'To visit Lelaanie.'

'Lelaanie is the past,' protested her mother harshly.

'It's my roots, Mom. The place where I was born. Where I lived for nearly seventeen years.'

'But now your life is here, in America. Philip's right, Teri. Use the money to buy a car. You've always wanted one.'

'It's eight years since we left the game park, and I want to see it again, Mom.'

'It's behind you, Teri. And anyway, even if you did go back, chances are you'd be disappointed. That's what happens when you return to places you loved when you were young.'

Teri drew a breath. Her stepfather noticed that in the last minute or so she had grown strangely pale.

'I want to see my grandfather.'

'Oh, lord... Teri, no!'

'I want so very much to see him. Please don't stop me, Mom.'

'I can't stop you. You're of age. And besides, it's your money.' Her mother's tone, usually so gentle, was unusually agitated. 'I can only tell you—it's not wise.'

'I don't agree.'

'As well as being disloyal.'

'No!'

'Disloyal? I don't understand,' Philip observed curiously. Once again he looked from his wife to his stepdaughter.

Odd, Teri thought, how much Philip doesn't know about us. Even after a year there are things he doesn't know.

'Mother figures that by going to visit my grandfather I'd be disloyal to my father's memory.'

'I know there was bad feeling...' Philip said carefully, obviously uncertain of his facts, and not sure how far he could go with them.

'It was very much more than bad feeling,' said Mary vehemently.

'You never talk about it, honey.'

'Only because it hurts too much.'

'Even now?'

'This last year with you, Philip, has been the best Teri and I have had since Tom died five years ago. You've made us both so happy. But when I think of Tom, and the way his life ended—and how it *didn't have to be*—then yes, it hurts even now.'

'You don't have to talk about it, honey.'

Mary glanced at Teri. 'I think I do.'

'You'll talk when you're ready.'

'I'm as ready today as I'll ever be. And if Teri's really serious about going off to Africa, then I think you should know what happened.'

'Mom...'

'Lelaanie is a private game park in the bushveld, Philip—that much you do know. Tom's father owned it.'

'Teri's grandfather,' Philip said.

'Teri's grandfather, yes. Stuart Masters. Man of the *bushveld*. Dedicated preserver of the wild. Tough as they come. Totally fearless. Man among men.'

'Don't be bitter, Mom, please,' Teri pleaded. 'It's all history now.'

'I'm just trying to paint a picture of your grandfather, Teri. Unless I do, how can Philip hope to understand?'

The look Philip directed towards his stepdaughter was compassionate. 'I'd like to understand, Teri.'

'Yes. OK...'

'Stuart Masters began life as a game ranger,' Mary went on. 'He was one of the best. Even as a young man, Tom used to tell me, people spoke of Stuart with awe. He was in his late twenties when he came into a great deal of money. An inheritance. Some of it he used to buy land. With the rest he sunk boreholes, cleared a road and built a house. More was added later. But that was the beginning of the game park that became Lelaanie.'

'Was Tom born already?' Philip asked.

'No. Stuart was in his mid-thirties when he married Beth, the daughter of another game ranger. By the time Tom was born, the game park was already becoming well-known.'

Mary looked at Philip. 'With such parents, you'd have thought Tom would have had the wild outdoor life in his blood. But Tom was different. Sensitive. Introspective. His parents' passion was the veld and the animals. Tom's passion was painting. Photography came after that.'

'Which led to conflict?'

'With a capital C. Only a tough outdoors man could win Stuart's respect. So you can imagine his contempt for Tom, who was the opposite of all he had wished for in a son. Still, things weren't too bad for Tom while his mother was alive. She was always there to make peace between her men. It was only later, after the car Beth was driving skidded off a flooded bridge, that life became intolerable.'

'Grandpa was beside himself with grief, Mom.' Though Teri had never known her grandmother, she was well acquainted with the story.

'That's true. Stuart adored Beth. But it didn't give him the right to treat Tom as he did. All the contempt he'd had for his son emerged at that point, Philip. Tom was dreadfully unhappy himself after his mother's death. He wanted to leave the veld and find consolation in his art, but the very idea was anathema to his father, who wanted to see his son a copy of himself.'

'One heck of a personality clash, obviously. I can see there'd be trouble,' Philip said quietly.

'For years Tom tried. Looking back now, I can't believe quite how long he tried to make a go of things at Lelaanie. When it all became too much for him, he'd take off and go to the cities for a while, and he'd spend his time at art exhibitions.'

'Which is how you met Dad,' Teri put in.

'At an exhibition, Teri, yes.' For a moment Mary's tone was soft with memory. 'But for the most part Tom's life was at the game park.'

'Lelaanie was your home after you were married?' Philip asked.

'For nearly eighteen years. Until the conflict between Tom and his father reached a peak. For years they'd bickered and fought. Stuart had a way of putting Tom down, of making him feel guilty and less than a man because he didn't have his father's toughness. One night there was a final argument. A dreadful argument. Tom told his father that he'd had enough, we were taking Teri and leaving Lelaanie. We were going to America, where Tom could make it in his own field.'

'How did Stuart Masters take it?'

'Very badly. He told Tom flatly that he would never make it, that he'd be a failure in America, just as he'd been at Lelaanie. That he'd come back penniless, and plead with his father to support us. It was a cruel, bitter argument. We left early the next day without even saying goodbye.'

'I said goodbye to Grandpa,' Teri said softly.

'I remember,' her mother said.

'And to Rafe,' Teri added.

'Rafe... Rafe Mathias. Good heavens, I haven't thought of him in years.' There was an odd look in the eyes that rested for a moment on Teri's face.

'Rafe?' Philip was curious.

'A young game ranger,' Mary told him. 'At least he was very young then. He'd be in his early thirties today, I suppose. Very good-looking, and almost as tough as Stuart himself. Well on the way to becoming Stuart's right-hand man.'

Philip happened to glance at Teri just then. The expression he saw in her face made him lead his wife back to her story. 'So you left Lelaanie and came to America.'

'And Tom tried to become an artist. As his father had predicted, he didn't make it. The American art world was too competitive for him, too sophisticated. He came into it far too late. He didn't have the right training.'

'Poor Tom.' There was compassion in Philip's tone.

'Poor Tom, yes. He had to see his lifelong dream come to nothing. Worse, he had to watch his family come close to poverty because there was no money coming in. It tore him apart, Philip. But he had to go on. And so he turned to his other love. Photography. And he began to make a living of sorts.'

'In all that time, did he never think of going back to Lelaanie?'

'Yes,' Mary said painfully. 'He did think of it. He even—and you may find this hard to believe—found himself missing Africa. But Tom was adamant that he would not go back without money, without a penny in his pocket. Not after all that had passed between his father and himself. Tom was a very proud man, Philip.'

'I can see that.'

'He became obsessed with the need to make money. It was an obsession that drove him to take terrible risks. He took photos that no one else would take because the risks were so great. Usually, those were the photos that brought in the most money. Again and again he put his life in danger for the sake of a picture.'

'Don't go on, Mom,' Teri pleaded. 'You don't have to put yourself through all this.'

'Teri's right, honey. I don't want you to upset yourself.'

'I *have* to go on. I've gone too far to stop now.' Mary took a jerky breath. 'One day Tom was photographing a man who was walking a tight rope stretched between two high buildings. The man made it, but Tom was perched on a window-ledge, and he lost his balance and fell.'

'That's appalling!' Philip's face was ashen.

Mary looked at him. 'Now do you see why I am so bitter about Stuart Masters? But for his treatment of his son, Tom would be alive today.'

For a long while there was silence in the room. The open bottle of champagne mocked them obscenely from its position on a small chrome and glass table. Mary's breath came in harsh gasps. Philip had his arm around her, he'd drawn her head into the curve of his throat. Teri wept softly.

At length Philip spoke. 'How did you cope afterwards?'

'You know that when I met you I had two jobs. While Teri was studying, she babysat, and on weekends she waitressed. That's the part you've always known, Philip.'

'Yes...'

'And then there was that other money,' Mary said musingly. 'An amount that came to us every month after Tom died. Regularly. Mysteriously. Without a name to it. Oh, I was able to guess who was sending it, but he never admitted to it.'

'*He*, Mary?'

'A man who admired Tom's daring. Kevin McGraw— it had to be him. A bit of an eccentric, I gather. I never knew him well myself. But Tom used to tell me about him. Lots of money, but no family of his own. I went to see him once—remember, Teri? He tried telling me he had nothing to do with it, he refused to accept my thanks. But I knew it had to be him, and I was grateful. Because of that money, Teri was able to go to college. We were able to live in a better neighbourhood. We were poor, but we never went hungry.'

'Quite a story,' Philip commented at last.

'You know all the rest of it.' Mary turned in his arm and looked up at him. For the first time there was the hint of a smile in her face. 'I met you, and we fell in love. And you've given Teri and me everything we could ever want.'

'Except very much in the way of money. I wish I could give you both more of that.'

'You've given us a loving home, Philip. That's all any woman really wants.'

Philip smiled down at his wife before bending his head to kiss her. It was just a light kiss, but Teri, feeling a bit of a spare wheel at that particular moment, stood up and went to the window.

The view of San Francisco had stunned her when they had first moved into this apartment. Even now, a year later, it never failed to hold her. But today Teri was thoughtful as she looked across the Golden Gate Bridge, free of mist for once, to the lights of Marin County.

For superimposed on the view before her eyes was another quite different, view. An endless vista of veld. Thorny trees and long wild grass swaying in the wind. A bearded man with faded blue eyes and a weathered face. And a younger man—as ruggedly tough as the older one.

It was Philip's voice which brought her back from the window. 'When were you planning on going to Africa, Teri?'

She turned, startled. 'I hadn't thought. I mean, after all that's just been said...'

But it was her mother who was silent, and Philip who spoke again, with immense gentleness. 'Teri's right about two things, Mary. She has her roots in Lelaanie. And the story—tragic though it is—is history now.'

Mary drew a shuddering breath. 'Yes...'

'You mean you wouldn't *mind* if I went back, Mom?' Teri asked incredulously.

'I would be a saint if I said I didn't mind. I do. But I feel a little better about it now. I should have told Philip the whole story a long time ago. I kept it all inside me for too long.'

'Oh, Mom!' Teri walked over to them both, and sat down on the floor at her mother's knees.

'I can see how much you want to go, darling. And Stuart *is* your grandfather.'

'I don't want to upset you.'

Mary stroked her hair. 'How long would you be gone?'

'I haven't thought that far ahead. It's all so new in my mind.'

'I guess you'd have to take leave from work,' said Philip.

'I do have three weeks due to me. I'll talk to Larry tomorrow. Perhaps he wouldn't mind if I took a fourth week unpaid.'

'We're talking a rich woman here,' Philip teased. 'It doesn't matter if she doesn't have money coming in for a week.'

A mild enough joke. But it lightened the tension in the room.

'I do have one favour to ask of you, Teri,' said her mother.

'Yes, of course.'

'I'd rather you didn't mention the lottery to your grandfather—or to anyone else, for that matter.'

'I won't if you don't want me to.'

'It's important to me. Vitally important. Think how humiliated your father would have been if your grandfather had ever learned the truth about our life in America.'

'You don't want Grandpa knowing that but for the lottery I could never have made the trip?'

'Exactly.'

Philip said, 'I don't think that's too much to ask, is it, Teri? In the circumstances?'

She smiled up at them both—at her mother who had given in so graciously, at Philip who had been her ally from the moment he had come into their lives. 'I won't say a word about the lottery. That's an absolute promise.'

'And perhaps you could get yourself a nice new wardrobe. Go to Lelaanie—Tom Masters' daughter—looking beautiful.'

'You know my weakness for clothes.' For the first time, Teri was able to laugh. 'It will be no great hardship for me to go out and splurge without feeling guilty.'

'You'll have so much to tell us when you get back,' Philip said.

'Yes! Golly, I'm so excited! Don't be hurt, Mom, but you know I always loved Lelaanie. The bushveld and the animals.'

'In that, you were always more like your grandfather than your father.'

'Rafe loved it all, too. Do you think he's still at Lelaanie?'

'I've no idea,' her mother said quietly. 'You mentioned him earlier, Teri. I remember you used to have a bit of a crush on Rafe'

'Was it that obvious?' Teri, who could normally take teasing in her stride, felt her cheeks redden.

'Only to me—because I'm your mother.'

'It was probably just a childhood thing. I mean, I was only just sixteen—well, nearly seventeen—the last time I saw him.'

'Are you still holding a torch for him, darling? Could Rafe be the reason you've never allowed yourself to get serious about a man?'

'Of course not,' Teri said, very firmly. 'In any case, he probably got married years ago, and doesn't even remember me.'

CHAPTER TWO

'NEXT stop is yours.'

'Yes! It's so weird to think I'm nearly there. I still can't believe it.'

'I love your American accent, and the words you use. Different from ours, aren't they?'

'Some of them.' Teri smiled at the woman who had been her travelling companion since the train had left Johannesburg several hours earlier. 'I guess I have become more American than I realised.'

'How long's it been since you were at Lelaanie?'

'Eight years.'

'That's a long time.'

'It seems like a lifetime.'

Teri turned her gaze from the woman back to the window. Friendly as her companion had been, in a sense she regretted not having had the compartment to herself for this trip back home. *Home*... Her mother might not like it, but home was how she thought of it right now, when she was so nearly there.

Emotion misted her eyes as she took in the passing countryside. The endless vistas of khaki bushveld. The lonely windmills, blades glinting in the sun. The acacias and the eucalyptus. Fields of mealies and tobacco. The herdboys with their cows and sheep. It was all so poignantly familiar, even after the many years away.

She was on her feet, suitcases beside her, as they pulled up at the next station. The train had not quite stopped when Teri opened the doors of the compartment, said goodbye to her travelling companion, and reached for her things.

The train stopped just long enough for Teri to disembark. Minutes later it was speeding down the tracks once more, and Teri was looking around her.

For the first time in four weeks she felt a little uncertain of herself. The tiny station, surrounded by eucalyptus and with the endless veld stretching away from it on all sides, was deserted. She had never doubted that someone—probably her grandfather—would be here to meet her. Now she wondered if she had been very stupid to make the assumption.

And then she saw a man coming around the station house. A tall, dark-haired man, with narrow hips and broad shoulders, his walk loose-limbed and easy. Everything about him suggested an enormous power and strength.

'Rafe!' She dropped her cases and ran to him. 'Oh, Rafe!'

She was about to fling her arms around his neck, but he seemed to step backwards beyond her reach, so that her arms never made it.

'Hello, Teri.'

'Rafe! Oh, Rafe, it's great to see you again!'

'That your luggage?'

She had been far too excited to make anything of the fact that he had side-stepped her attempted embrace. But the abruptness of his words was unexpected and chilling. Her arms dropped to her side as she looked up at him.

There was an aloofness in the handsome rugged face. A sternness which she did not remember.

'Rafe?' she whispered.

Hooded brown eyes regarded her steadily from beneath dark, well-defined eyebrows. Over high cheekbones, the tanned skin was taut. 'Those *are* your things?'

She began to tremble. 'I've been away eight years, Rafe.'

'Eight and a half. I can count too, Teri.'

'Whatever. It doesn't really matter. What kind of welcome is this?'

He shrugged. 'I take it you weren't expecting a red carpet and a bouquet of roses.'

'Red carpet and roses? What are you saying? Why are you so sarcastic? I'm so happy to see you. So excited. Aren't you at all happy to see me?'

Something flickered in the dark eyes that swept her face, lingering just for a moment on trembling lips which had once been crushed beneath his. It had been an embrace which a desperately unhappy teenage girl had relived over and over again in those first lonely months in America.

'What do you want me to say, Teri?'

'Forget it, Rafe.' Her voice was hard now. 'I'd hate you to say anything you didn't want to.'

Abruptly she turned so that he would not see the glimmer of tears in her eyes. She jerked her head in the direction of her luggage. 'Yes—those are mine.'

Easily he picked up the heavy cases. Without a word, he started walking along the platform. After a moment, Teri followed him. She did not wait for Rafe to open the passenger door of the jeep, but opened it herself and climbed inside as Rafe put in her suitcases.

'We're driving straight to Lelaanie?' she asked, as they left the station.

'Yes. Unless there's somewhere else you wanted to go first.'

'Of course not. I'm longing to see my grandfather.'

'Ah . . .' Said so strangely.

'He does know I'm coming, doesn't he?'

'He's thought of little else since you wrote to him.' Rafe's voice was dry.

'Does that mean he's pleased?'

'He's overjoyed.' The dryness was even more pronounced.

'But you're not as pleased to see me back, are you, Rafe?'

He shrugged. 'I didn't say that.'

He didn't have to. His manner said it for him. Feeling a little ill, Teri turned her eyes away from the man she'd once imagined herself in love with, and watched the scenery. At first it was all very much like the farming countryside which she'd glimpsed from the train. But after a while it became wilder, less civilised, as cultivated fields gave way to windswept, long-grassed bushveld.

Teri knew she was in game-park country when she saw a small herd of grazing impala. About to ask Rafe if he would stop the jeep, she bit her lips on the question. With the old Rafe she would have had no qualms. This new Rafe was a remote stranger. She had a feeling there were things one did not ask him.

For more than an hour they drove with hardly a word between them. Rafe switched on the radio, and Teri was glad of the country music that filled the car. The strain was beginning to get to her.

It was only when the great stone gates of Lelaanie came into sight that she turned to Rafe, unable to hide her excitement.

'I can't believe it—we've arrived. We've actually arrived!'

'That we have.'

She wanted to shake him. But she said nothing as he slowed the jeep to the snail's pace that was a basic regulation of all game parks. And in a short time she ceased to think of Rafe. Sitting forward in her seat, she looked out of the front window, gripped by an old and familiar thrill as her eyes combed the bush.

'A dollar for the one who spots the first elephant?' she suggested, going back to a joke that went back many years.

'We don't use American currency here, Teri.'

She did not look at him. 'My mistake. Sorry. I just thought you'd remember our old game.'

Rafe did not answer. And Teri, deciding that she would not let him affect her homecoming, just went on searching the bush with her eyes.

There were animals. Not very many, but each one, after all this time, was a thrill. Two warthogs waddling awkwardly into the bush. A bright-hued bird calling to its mate. A troop of monkeys making obscene gestures from the side of the road.

Teri could not help laughing at the monkeys. 'If we stopped the car they'd be all over the hood in a moment.'

'*Hood*, Teri?'

It took her a few moments to think of the word she had once used. 'Bonnet?'

'Yes,' Rafe said. 'They'd be all over the bonnet.'

'Nothing's changed,' she said softly.

'You're naïve if you think that.'

Teri turned in her seat. 'I know that you've changed.'

'Perhaps I have.'

'I've yet to find out why.'

But if she had sought to disconcert him she had not succeeded. The eyes that met hers were hard to read. It was so much easier to look at the bush. At the trees and the grasses, at the animals, all of which seemed to be as old as Africa itself.

She found herself saying, 'It's really weird, Rafe. So many memories suddenly taking shape before my eyes.'

'How much do you remember, Teri?' He did not sound quite so aloof now.

'Everything.'

'Everything?' For the first time there was the hint of a smile in his voice. 'You're sure of that?'

'Quite sure.'

Turning from the window once more, she looked at him. She'd wondered sometimes whether the feelings of a sixteen-year-old could have played tricks with her. Whether Rafe Mathias had really been as dynamic as she remembered him. She saw now that her youthful instincts had played her true, for Rafe was still the most attractive man she'd ever met. What disturbed her was his manner. 'I'll prove it to you,' she said. 'Those mopanis up on the hill. There's a clearing just beyond them. There'll be impalas grazing there.'

'You could be right.'

He was laughing. The sound seemed to find its way straight to her heart-strings, tugging hard at them.

She kept her voice firm. 'And half a mile further on we'll get to the ghost trees.'

'Yes, they're still there.'

'Petrified as ever?' Another old saying which they had made their own.

'As ever. With a couple of new ones added to them.'

'What about the hollow baobab tree? Is it still home to an elephant?'

Again he laughed. 'It never was, Teri. That was just one of the things you liked to tell yourself.'

'You'll never convince me of that.' Now that she had a conversation going, Teri was determined not to let it flag. 'Talking of elephants, I guess Young Rascal is still laying down the law.'

'Young Rascal is quite old now, Teri.'

'I don't believe it!'

'Ivory poachers got to him. He was never the same again after that.'

'That's terrible! Poaching is still a problem, then, Rafe?'

'Just one of our problems,' he said grimly.

'I want to hear about all of them.'

'I doubt you'll have time for that in a four-week visit. Much less the interest.'

She put a quick hand on his arm. 'Rafe, don't.' Beneath her fingers she felt his muscles stiffen, but she went on, nevertheless. 'I don't know what's bugging you, but I wish you wouldn't shut me out. Please!'

'Look, Teri, your impala,' he pointed out without expression.

A little bewildered, she followed his gaze. She saw that they were passing the clearing she had spoken of just minutes before, but suddenly it didn't mean all that much to her.

'You haven't told me anything about my grandfather,' she said now.

'I don't remember that you asked.'

Teri dug her nails into the soft palms of her hands. 'I thought he might be at the station.'

'No, Teri, I don't think you really thought that.'

Something in his tone got to her. 'Why not?'

Rafe was silent a moment. At length he said, 'I will say this—you've chosen quite a time for your visit.'

'What do you mean?'

'You'll see when you meet your grandfather. You and the rest of your clan, who are all so busy remembering him now.'

Fear curled in her chest. 'What do you mean, Rafe? Is Grandpa ill?'

'I'm sure I don't have to tell you. You know it already. Which is why you decided to come.'

'Rafe! You're frightening me.'

'Don't play this game of being innocent with me, Teri.' His tone was thick with contempt.

'Grandpa *is* ill, then?'

He looked at her coldly. 'Yes, Teri, he's ill.'

They had gone a mile or two further when Rafe said, 'By the way, I was very sorry about your father.'

'Yes...'

'Did he never think of coming back to Lelaanie?'

'I don't think so.'

'America proved to be all he hoped it would be?'

Fiercely loyal to her mother's wishes, and to the father she had loved so much, Teri said, 'Dad was a successful man.'

And that, she decided, was no more than the truth. Tom Masters had been true to himself and the ideals he'd valued and believed in. His wife and daughter had adored him, and he had made them both happy.

'Your grandfather always thought he would be back.'

'Because he didn't believe that Dad could make it in a different world from his own.'

'Yet it's obvious he did. I've only to look at the expensive clothes you're wearing. Your luggage. He must have made a lot of money.'

'Dad needed to live his own life,' Teri said carefully.

'Of course,' Rafe said grimly.

'He had a right to that.'

'I'm not saying he didn't. But he could have tried to make things up.'

'Grandpa could have tried too.'

'Your grandfather is an old man, Teri. Why didn't your father ever think of coming for a visit? As for you— you could have been back yourself before now. You did say...' He stopped, and it was as if he had deliberately checked himself. 'Why did you wait so long?' he asked then.

'I don't want to think about the could-haves,' she said, again remembering the promise she had made to her mother. 'I'm here now, and I mean to make the most of my trip.'

The thatched roofs of the camp rondavels were in sight when Teri dared to ask the one question that had been on her mind from the moment she had decided to go back to Lelaanie.

'I guess you're married now, Rafe.' Her voice was light.

The strong long-fingered hands tightened for an instant on the steering-wheel, and in the hard line of the jaw something seemed to move. But when Rafe answered his tone was perfectly calm. 'No.'

Teri experienced a moment of pure joy. An unreasonable joy, really, in light of Rafe's obvious dislike of her.

And then he said, 'I was engaged once. But I broke it off because...'

'Why?'

'Because I...' He stopped.

'Because?' she prompted.

The closed look deepened. 'It's history now, Teri. It doesn't matter any more.' He reached for her left hand, turning it over in his own hand. 'What about you? I don't see a ring.'

The touch of his hand on hers set unexpected fires flaming all the way up her arm. But she managed to say, very steadily, 'I'm not married either.'

'You're a very beautiful woman, Teri. Has there never been a man in your life?'

'One man, yes.' She withdrew her hand from his. 'And now I want to see my grandfather. Please take me to him, Rafe.'

Teri was shocked at her first sight of Stuart Masters. For several stunned moments she could scarcely believe that the frail man who smiled so tremulously as he held out his hands to her, could really be the person she had travelled so far to see. She glanced as if for confirmation at a stony-faced Rafe, who gave the slightest of nods. So great was her shock that she felt her legs weaken beneath her.

But Teri was a courageous girl. In seconds she had herself under control. And then she was at her grandfather's side, bending her head to kiss him as she took his hands in hers.

'Grandpa! It's wonderful to see you.'

'Not as wonderful as it is to see you, *liefie*,' he said, using the local endearment by which he had called her all her growing-up years.

Incredibly, she saw that Stuart Masters, who had been every bit the tough man her mother had described him, had tears in his eyes.

'It's been a long time, Grandpa.'

'Too long, *liefie*.'

She managed to hide her own tears as she gently stroked the paper-thin hands. 'I'm here now.'

'I never gave up hope that you would come, Teri. I always told you she would come one day, didn't I, Rafe?'

'You did say it,' came the terse acknowledgement.

'How you've changed, *liefie*. You left here a child. Not quite seventeen. And you've come back a woman. Isn't she beautiful, Rafe?'

'Yes, Stuart, she's very beautiful.'

But when Teri looked quickly round at Rafe the eyes that met hers were sardonic. He'd agreed with her grandfather only because he knew it was expected of him. Teri felt her cheeks redden.

She was relieved when Rafe said, 'If you don't mind, I'll leave the two of you alone together for a while. I know you've things to talk about.'

'And I'm sure you must have things to do before nightfall,' Teri said.

'Yes, as a matter of fact I do have things to do.'

It was said so drily that Teri, looking at him once more, wondered why everything she said seemed to create sparks. She was glad when Rafe left the room.

'Come sit by me, Teri.'

There was a chair in the corner of the room, and Teri drew it up beside her grandfather. Close enough so that she could take his hands in hers once more.

'I just want to look at you,' he said.

While he was looking at her, she was looking at him too, and feeling distressed by what she saw. To Teri, her grandfather had always seemed ageless. It was very difficult to accept the change she saw in him.

'Are you well, Grandpa?' she asked softly, knowing full well that he was not.

'I passed my allotted years a long time ago.'

'You're not answering my question.'

'I will in a while, *liefie*. There are other things to talk about first. So many things.'

'Yes...'

'You remind me so much of your father. The same eyes. The tilt of your lips when you smile.'

'People have said we were alike.'

'I was a stubborn old fool, Teri.'

'I don't want you to distress yourself, Grandpa.'

'It has to be said. All those arguments we had. Always because I wanted Tom to be something he could never be.'

'Grandpa, please...'

'Don't you see, Teri, I have to say it? I was wrong, *liefie*. Tom was an artist. I should have let him paint. He was never like me. Like Rafe. I saw Rafe growing up to be the man I had always wanted Tom to be. Hard, tough, independent. Loving the veld and the animals as I do. And it hurt me that my son was so different.'

'We can't change the way we are,' Teri said quietly.

'I learned that too late. From the day Tom died I have lived with my regrets. Your mother wrote and told me about the accident, did you know that? And I kept hoping she would bring you home to Lelaanie.'

'I think Dad wanted us to make America our home.'

'Teri—I have to know, was your father happy?'

'Yes, he was. He was doing what he wanted.'

'You always loved your parents. You've been a loyal daughter, Teri.'

She was caught by something in his tone. 'What makes you say that?'

'Isn't that what you are?'

She looked away. Her grandfather couldn't possibly know of the promise she'd made to her mother. It was just his peculiar use of words that had got to her.

'Mother has remarried,' she told him. 'Her husband's name is Philip Willis. He's not my father, he can never replace him, but he's a good man.'

'I'm glad. Your mother deserves some happiness.'

'I also wish things could have been different,' she said in a low voice.

'Maybe it's not too late.' His hand moved in hers. 'You don't know how much this visit means to me, Teri. How long will you be here?'

'Four weeks.'

'Just four weeks...?'

'We'll make the most of every day.'

Stuart Masters was silent, almost as if he had withdrawn into himself to a place where Teri could not reach him. She wondered what he was thinking.

At length he said, 'You asked if I was well. I don't have much time left to me, *liefie*.'

'Don't say that!'

'I'm an old rogue, and I've led a darned good life.' It was his turn to stroke her hand. 'But it would mean a lot to me if you could just stay here with me a little longer.'

'Oh, Grandpa!' Her throat was choked with tears, so that she couldn't go on.

'When your letter came, it was the miracle I had prayed for.'

'I wish I could have come earlier.'

'Perhaps it wasn't possible. Anyway, you are right, *liefie*. We'll just have to make the most of each day we have.'

Teri saw that her grandfather's eyes were beginning to look heavy with fatigue. Gently, she said that she would leave him alone for a while so that he could nap. She would visit him again later.

The sun was beginning to set as she left the master rondavel which Stuart Masters had shared with his Beth so many years ago. It occurred to Teri that she had not yet seen anything of Lelaanie, for upon her arrival she had gone immediately to her grandfather. But, much as she wanted to reacquaint herself with the camp compound, she was in no mood to look around now.

Almost without thinking she walked past the bougainvillaea-covered rondavels towards the spot that had been her haven from the time she was little. The stone bench was where it had always been, behind the camp wall. It was set high, on a piece of sloping ground, so that even if you were sitting back against it you could see over the top of the wall, across the river and into the bush. But, though it was high, it was also secluded. People who did not know about the bench could spend a week at Lelaanie and never see it.

The veld was broodingly mysterious beneath the last rays of the afternoon sun. A little way downstream a few kudu were drinking, unperturbed by the cheeky monkeys swinging and screaming in the trees. Further on, a few zebra emerged from the bush and began to make their way towards the water.

Teri watched the tranquil scene for a few moments. And then, as she felt the tears she had managed to keep at bay during her visit with her grandfather come suddenly to the surface, she put her hands over her eyes and wept.

It was only when a familiar voice said, 'Here you are, Teri,' that she dropped her hands and looked up.

'Hi,' she said in a muffled voice, as she dug around in the pocket of her jacket for a tissue to wipe her eyes.

'You never did carry the necessities of life around with you.'

Rafe sounded amused as he withdrew a tissue from his own pocket, and touched her eyes with it.

'Last time we were together you dried my tears for me, too.' She wasn't sure what made her say it, except perhaps that the last half-hour had made her feel very vulnerable.

'You have a good memory,' he said drily.

'We were here, on this same bench, and I was crying because I couldn't bear to leave Lelaanie. And...' She almost stopped. But in the end she added, 'I hated saying goodbye to you, Rafe.'

She thought Rafe made a noise in his throat, but she couldn't be sure. And then he had moved away from her, and was standing at the wall with his back to her, his hands shoved deep into the pockets of his jeans.

She had a great urge to go up to him and put her arms around his waist and lean her cheek against his back. Something had happened to make Rafe turn against her, and she hated him for the way he was behaving. Yet at the same time the old attraction was still there, so that she knew why she had never allowed herself to get too close to any man in all the years in America.

'And today, Teri... What made you cry today?' He still had his back to her.

'Wishing that things could have been different. That two stubborn men who must have loved each other once could have found a way of getting together.'

'That's it?'

'That—and just being with my grandfather. Seeing how frail he is.'

'Come on, Teri,' Rafe said impatiently, swinging around to look at her.

'He's so changed, Rafe.'

'You knew he would be.'

'Not like this.'

'Come on, Teri,' he said again.

'If I thought about it at all, I knew he would be eight years older than when I'd last seen him. But Grandpa was always so—indestructible. It tears me apart to see him like this.'

'You mean that's why you were crying?' Even in the fading light she could see that his expression was one of contempt.

'Yes.'

'I find that very hard to believe,' he said, with even greater impatience this time. 'You could have come to visit years ago, but no, you had to wait until now. When...' He stopped. When he went on, his tone was harsh. 'Don't play on my sympathy, Teri. You could do that once, when you were very young and lovely, and I believed there wasn't a trace of duplicity in you. But not now.'

Towering above her, he was more than ever a superb giant of a man. His head was held proudly above the powerful thrust of his throat, and beneath a tight shirt and jeans he was all steely muscle. No woman could look at him and fail to be touched by the powerful force of his sexuality.

But Teri was in no mood to assess his attractiveness. 'You've absolutely no right to talk to me like this!' She was shaking with outrage.

'I've every right, Teri, and you'd better believe that. I'm the one who was at your grandfather's side all these years, while you never gave him a thought.'

'You're so sure of yourself, aren't you?' she said tautly.

'I've no reason not to be.'

'You're determined to think the worst of me. Why?'

'Put it down to cynicism.'

'You never used to be cynical, Rafe.'

'We all change.'

After a moment she asked, 'Do you see changes in me?'

'You've changed so much that I barely recognise you. Your clothes, your accent. The words you use. You've become American, Teri.'

'I suppose I have,' she conceded slowly. 'In eight years that was inevitable. But these changes you talk of, they're only external. I'm still the same person I was when I left Lelaanie.'

'No,' he said flatly. 'I don't know you at all.'

His words were like knives, each one stabbing her where she was most vulnerable. Relentless, wounding. And somehow unreasonable. Rafe was an angry, bitter man, but Teri had still to understand why. The fact that she had taken so long to return to Lelaanie could not be sufficient reason in itself.

'You came here looking for me, didn't you?' she asked at last, deciding it was time to change the subject.

'It's getting dark. And it's almost time for supper.'

'You knew where to come.'

He shrugged. 'The compound's not all that big.'

'Nobody ever used this bench. Nobody except me. And sometimes both of us.'

He moved his feet on the dry sand. 'What are you getting at now?'

'I'm just remembering that last time we were here together. When you dried my tears.'

'Don't go on with this,' he ordered abruptly.

'Do you remember what happened after that?' she persisted softly.

'Haven't a clue.'

'You took me in your arms, Rafe. You drew me on to your lap and you held me very tightly, and then you kissed me.'

'If that's what happened—and I do say *if*—then it was because you were distressed. You were leaving Lelaanie with your folks the next morning.'

'I was kissing you back, Rafe. I've never forgotten it.'

'I was just comforting you, Teri.'

'At least you're admitting to it. But it was more than just comfort.'

'You're mistaken.'

'Do you think I could forget the way the way you held me?'

'Good grief! What is this?' He took a step backwards. 'Is this how you try to seduce all the men you meet in America?'

She decided to let that one pass. Instead she said, 'From the moment I arrived here today you've been unpleasant. Why, Rafe? *Why?* Do you really hate me so much?'

His eyebrows lifted. 'Hate implies an intensity of emotion. I don't feel any emotion for you, Teri.'

'Except contempt.'

'Maybe.'

She couldn't carry on with the conversation, it just hurt too much.

'It's getting late,' he said. 'You'll want to wash before supper.'

'Wait.' She put her hand on his arm. 'Before we go back, tell me about my grandfather. How is he? And please don't put me off by saying I know it all already.'

'All right, then.' There was pain in Rafe's voice. 'He's been very ill.'

'He told me,' Teri said in a choked voice, 'that he doesn't have much time left.'

'I think that could be true.'

'How long? You have to tell me.'

'We don't know. A few months, maybe.'

'Oh, lord!' It was an anguished cry. 'If only Dad had been able to... If I could have...'

Seeking comfort, she thrust herself at Rafe, ignoring the way he stiffened against her.

'Hold me, Rafe,' she wept. 'Please hold me.'

'No!' His breathing was ragged as his arms lifted, only to drop as they were about to close around her. 'You have to stop this, Teri.'

But she was desperate for comfort. Her arms were around his neck, holding him tightly. Her behaviour was unthinking, born of an intensity of grief.

'Hold me,' she sobbed. 'Why won't you hold me?'

He seemed to make one final effort to resist her. And then his arms did go around her, crushing her against him as his head came down to hers. There was no tenderness in his kiss. Just a passion compounded of anger and despair. Savagely he kissed her, hungrily. As if he'd been waiting for years to do just this, and couldn't get enough of it.

As sanity suddenly returned, Teri was confused by the sheer depth of his emotion. His kisses were sparking flames through all the nerves of her body, making her wish for more. And yet, as his kisses deepened, becoming even hungrier and more possessive, she knew instinctively that something was very wrong.

From somewhere she found the strength to thrust her hands between their bodies so that she could push him away. Vainly she tried to twist her lips away from his punishing mouth, but for half a minute at least he went on kissing her.

'No!' she got out, as he stopped once to draw breath.

For the first time he seemed to register her distress. Puzzled, he looked down at her.

'Isn't this what you wanted?' The question emerged on a shuddering breath.

'No.' She was trembling, and very close to tears once more. 'I never wanted it to be like this.'

'You don't know what the hell you want,' he ground out harshly.

Pushing her out of his arms, so abruptly that she could have fallen, he strode away in the gathering darkness.

Feeling utterly shaken, Teri watched him go. And she realised that she knew exactly what it was that she wanted from Rafe Mathias.

CHAPTER THREE

NEXT day Teri made two long-distance phone calls from the office at Lelaanie. Both were to San Francisco.

The first call was to her mother. Mary Willis was shocked to hear Teri's voice. Bitter as she had been about Tom's father in recent years, she had not always felt this way. There had been affection between them once.

'It's just as well you went to Lelaanie when you did, honey. You were right and I was wrong.'

'Oh, Mom! You don't know how relieved I am to hear you say that.'

'It must mean a lot to your grandfather to see you again.'

'So much that...' Teri hesitated, then pressed on. 'I've decided to stay on here.'

'Permanently?' Mary's startled voice crackled through the line.

'No, of course not. I'm just thinking of extending my trip a bit. I know I was thinking of four weeks, but since I do have an open ticket, I can fly back home whenever I like.'

'As long as it's within the year.'

Teri clutched the phone so tightly that her knuckles were white. 'If Rafe is right, it might not be more than a few months.'

'So Rafe is still there,' Mary said. And then, 'I don't know what to say, Teri.'

'I hope you'll give me your blessing.' Teri took a breath. 'Grandpa is desperately sorry that he didn't make his peace with Dad. I know it's a little late for regrets, but there it is. Anyway, I really feel I should stay.'

Mary took a moment to answer. Teri clutched the phone even more tightly. Then she heard her mother say, 'You're probably doing the right thing.'

'You don't know how much it means to me to hear you say that.'

'Teri,' there was a new note in her mother's voice, 'you haven't said anything to Stuart about the lottery?'

Teri thought of Rafe, and of how he took it for granted that her family would have been financially secure enough for her to have returned to Lelaanie a long time ago.

'No.'

'About us having no money?'

'I made you a promise, and I mean to keep it.'

'I know you will.'

'Give Philip a hug for me.'

'He's right here, and he sends one back to you. And, Teri, give...give your grandfather my love, will you?'

Teri's other call was to her employer. After graduating from college several years earlier, she had gone to work for Larry Anderson, who headed a small company which made films for the educational and travel markets. With her own educational background in history and communications, Teri had quickly become invaluable to Larry. He often called her his Girl Friday, and in fact she really did do something of everything for him. She was a whiz at research. Her marketing skills were excellent. And she was never averse to helping out in the secretarial department when that was what was needed.

'Take as long as you need,' was his immediate response when he heard the situation she'd found herself in.

'You really mean that, Larry?'

'Sure do, honey.'

'Won't it be hard for you without me there for so long?'

'Devastating. But knowing you, I figure you'll do whatever you need to anyway, even if I'm not crazy about it. I'll just have to find some good temporary help. Probably need three people to do the work you do on your own.'

'Larry, you're an absolute darling.'

'I wish you'd give me some tangible proof of that sometimes.'

'You know I'm not that kind of girl,' she came back laughingly.

'To my cost,' was the rueful answer.

Over the years Teri and Larry had developed an easy relationship—part teasing, part flirtatious, yet businesslike at the same time. Larry, who had been divorced before Teri had met him, made no secret of the fact that he found her attractive, and now and then she had given in to his pleading and gone out with him.

But, apart from the fact that she had no deep feelings for him, Teri knew that Larry did not have it in him to be a one-woman man, and she had always been careful not to let herself get serious about him. They would never be more than friends, and they both realised it. Which did not stop him from flirting with her.

'Listen,' he was saying now, 'out there in the boonies you might even come up with some good ideas we could use.'

'It's quite possible.'

'More than possible. Hey, Teri, YZ Productions were given the final go-ahead on the game-park assignment.'

'Really?'

'They're going out to Southern Africa quite soon. I'd willingly give an arm to be involved in that one. You might even run into Archie Logan and the rest of the gang.'

'Somehow I think it's unlikely.'

'You never know. Anyway, you just enjoy your visit with your grandfather. And don't worry about your job. I'll keep it safe for you.'

'I don't know how to thank you.'

He laughed again. 'We'll find a way. Just remember that you owe me one now, Teri.'

She was laughing, too. 'You're a darling, Larry. An absolute darling.'

'Things aren't the same without you here. I miss you already, honey.'

'I miss you too, Larry.'

Stuart Masters was visibly moved when Teri told him of her decision to extend her trip.

'All these years I've wondered what Beth would have said if she'd known the mess I made of things.'

'I think Grandma would have forgiven you,' Teri said softly.

'Never! She'd have been furious. She had a tongue on her, that woman. But now... with you here, I've felt I've been given another chance. You are the future, Teri.'

They were in his rondavel, where he kept all his precious things within reach. The field-glasses which he'd used all his adult life to scour the bush for game. A battered, wide-brimmed felt hat. A folder filled with yellowed newspaper cuttings telling of the exploits of the young Stuart Masters, the daringly courageous game warden.

Photographs in old-fashioned frames stood on the table beside his bed. A wedding photo—a dashing young man and his pretty bride. Other photos, with the bride and groom grown older, but still good-looking, with laughing eyes and strong faces. Only one person was missing from the group.

But Teri's grandfather was reaching for a photo album as he said, 'Come sit by me, Teri. It's a while since I've looked at these.'

And there, in the album, were photos of Teri's father, Tom, a freckle-faced child with dreamy eyes.

'Such a waste,' Stuart Masters muttered.

'We'll look at them again another time, Grandpa.' Teri was concerned at seeing him looking so sad.

'Another time. Yes.' He raised himself suddenly in his chair. 'You haven't seen anything of Lelaanie, Teri. The park itself.'

'I saw a bit on the way in from the station.'

'You have to see it all. We'll get the jeep. I'll drive you around.'

'I'll drive her,' a low voice said.

Teri spun around at the same time as her grandfather looked towards the door.

'I'm taking the jeep out anyway,' Rafe said, but Teri sensed that he made the comment only because he did not want her grandfather to exert himself.

'You'll show her everything, Rafe?'

'Of course I will. And now it's time you got some rest, Stuart.'

Outside the rondavel, Teri said, 'You really don't have to do this.'

'Don't I?' he asked sardonically.

'Of course not.'

'Don't kid yourself, Teri. Your grandfather will want to know exactly what you saw. Besides——' he grinned down at her suddenly '—I've never been averse to showing beautiful women around Lelaanie.'

'Well, OK then,' she said lightly enough, hating the impersonal way he had fitted her into some general category, yet wise enough not to say so.

The camp was very quiet at this time of the morning. Many of the guests were already out with the guides. They had left at the first light of dawn, when the animals were waking from sleep and on their way to the waterholes to drink.

As they left the camp compound, Teri was disturbingly aware of Rafe's closeness on the seat beside her, stirred by the long, lean body just inches away from her; the powerful arms, the taut thighs, the clean male smell that filled her nostrils.

She had to force her eyes away from him and to the window. No good letting herself think too much about Rafe. Not this new Rafe, who did not seem to like her at all.

'Remember how to search for animals, Teri?' she heard him ask after a while.

She turned her eyes back to him. 'Some things you never forget. Middle distance, Rafe.'

'Middle distance,' he agreed, with the smile in his voice which she'd heard only once or twice yesterday.

'Anything by the roadside you can't miss. And if there's an animal on the horizon it'll be too far away for you to see it decently anyway.' She looked at him. 'Do you remember teaching me that?'

'If I did, you were a good student.'

'There's not much I've forgotten about that time,' she said softly, her eyes on the handsome profile.

She wondered if he would rise to her bait, but not a muscle moved. Instead he said, 'Teri, look.'

'Where?'

'Behind the mopanis. There...in the bend of the road.'

'I don't see a thing...' She was frowning as her eyes concentrated on the trees. For a moment she was sure Rafe was just kidding her because she'd been so busy talking instead of looking for game.

And then suddenly she exclaimed, 'Yes!'

'You see it?'

'Oh, yes! A bit of movement. Grey...'

'And you know what it is?'

'An elephant,' she exclaimed breathlessly. 'Right, Rafe, it is an elephant, isn't it?'

'Right.'

'Oh, Rafe! So close to camp. It's an omen, I know it is.'

'You were always one for omens.' He was laughing. 'Haven't you outgrown them by now?'

'I guess not. Please, let's stop.'

'We will, but we'll pass it first. You can't have forgotten that it's always best to have an elephant behind rather than in front of you, so that it can't cut off your means of escape.'

Very slowly Rafe passed the mopanis before bringing the car to a stop. They might have to wait some time before the elephant came into full view, but he kept the engine running anyway. Where there were elephants there could be surprises, and it was always best to be ready for a quick get-away.

As it was, they did not have long to wait. With a great flapping of ears the elephant emerged from the trees and into the middle of the road. There it stopped and looked straight at the car. Menacingly it lifted its ears and trunk and let out a huge bellow.

Winding down her window—the thing Rafe had always warned her not to do—Teri gazed out entranced. The elephant planted a giant wrinkled foot a step nearer to the car, and bellowed again.

Teri was wondering if the elephant meant to charge, when it suddenly seemed to lose interest in the car, and ambled over the road and into the bush. Moments later it was lost from sight, with the crashing of branches the only reminder that it had been there.

'What a splendid creature!' Teri turned shining eyes to Rafe. 'That's what Africa is to me. That prehistoric monster crashing through the bush.'

Rafe's answering look was amused. 'Something in your face tells me you'd forgotten.'

'Not forgotten. I could *never* forget. In those first years I used to dream about Lelaanie. And about...' She stopped the last thought very firmly.

'I hear a but.'

'In my daily life in San Francisco—you'd have to see San Francisco to know what I mean, Rafe—I'd have been taken for crazy or drunk, or both, if I'd said I saw an elephant walk out of the bush.'

He laughed. 'I suppose so.'

For the first time he was looking relaxed. In the bush, in his own world, Rafe was at last the man Teri remembered.

They drove on, taking a road northwards, a different road from the one they had travelled along yesterday. Teri needed no help in spotting game now. If there were animals on her side of the road she saw them. And sometimes—with the return of a strange sixth sense— she even knew when there was something on Rafe's side.

Zebra and wildebeest grazed in separate groups yet in a traditional togetherness a few miles further on. The zebra, wild and strong and beautiful, looked at the car a few moments before sprinting off into the bush.

And then there were giraffe, majestically aloof as they nibbled from the tallest trees. And water buck, white rings circling their rear ends.

And always, wherever they went, impala, delicate and lovely. 'They look as if they've just stepped out of a bath,' Teri said.

'Now where have I heard that one before?' Rafe teased.

'You'll say next that I haven't changed in eight years. Am I really so boring?'

The deliberately provocative question had been a mistake, for the amusement had vanished from Rafe's eyes as he turned a cynical look her way.

'You've changed, Teri. I told you that yesterday. And no, you're not boring. You never were.'

Teri felt her cheeks redden. Uncertain how to answer what sounded like a rather double-edged observation, she turned away from Rafe once more.

They drove further north, with Teri growing first puzzled, then increasingly tense, at what she was seeing. But she said nothing until Rafe stopped the car at a look-out point situated on a high kopje. It was a place where people were allowed to leave their vehicles if they were in the company of a guide.

She felt quite safe as she and Rafe got out of the jeep and walked along the path that led to the top of the kopje. Rafe, who was familiar with every square inch of the game park, knew what he was doing.

Reaching the edge of the look-out point, Rafe turned to Teri. There was an odd expression in his face as he offered her his binoculars. 'Care to look?'

'Thanks.'

It took her a few moments to adjust the glasses to her eyes. Then she was sweeping the landscape with them, taking in an endless vista of veld. Nothing moved. Not an animal, not even a bird. No matter which way Teri directed her gaze, the view was always the same. Mile upon mile of parched and dying scrub.

Her face was white when she put the binoculars from her eyes. 'This is awful, Rafe!'

'You noticed.' His voice was grim.

'I've been noticing for some time now. The dying grass. The sick-looking trees. I kept hoping it was just some isolated patch we were passing through.'

'Now you know differently.'

'Yes.'

Teri's gaze encompassed the huge circle of veld stretching to the horizon. 'I can't believe this. It all used to be so lush. What's happened here?'

'Drought.'

'Oh, dear heaven!'

'You must have known about it. Even as far as away as the city of the Golden Gate Bridge, you must have heard about the terrible African drought.' His voice was as dry as the landscape.

'Yes, of course.'

'Why are you so surprised, then?'

She made a helpless gesture. 'I never imagined it could be as bad as this at Lelaanie.'

'Didn't you?'

'It looks—as if the very life-blood has been squeezed out of the veld.'

'There was a time when it was very much worse than this.'

She looked at him, taking in the lines that ran deep in the tanned face. 'I don't know why, but I thought there'd been rain in recent years.'

'You're right, the drought did break, but there are huge areas where, when the rain did come, it was a case of too little, too late.'

She blinked away tears. 'And yet there are other areas, too. Veld where the animals *can* find water and pasture. I saw them yesterday. And when we first left camp this morning.'

'There's been localised rain this year and last, Teri. Very good rain sometimes. That's where the veld looks healthy. When the guides take out the guests, they stick to those areas.'

'And then there's this.'

'This is just a small part of it.'

'Has it been very bad for the animals?' she asked in a small voice.

'I'm afraid so.' Rafe's face looked even grimmer now. 'We do what we can. We create new waterholes to take the place of the pools that are dry. But even then there are problems. Some of it's hellish, like at...' He stopped.

'Like at?' she prompted.

'Forget it.'

'No! Please tell me.'

'Forget it, I said.'

'I want to know. To see.'

'It's not a pretty sight, Teri.'

'I can take it.'

He looked down at her, his eyes hard. 'You'll never see anything like it in San Francisco.'

'Show me all the same,' she insisted. 'Grandpa asked you to show me everything.'

'Not the parts I'm thinking of,' he muttered.

With a sudden flash of insight, Teri asked, 'Does he know they exist?'

Abruptly Rafe moved away from her. Teri watched him tensely. A tall, superbly built figure standing at the very edge of the look-out point. Rigidity in every muscle of his body, from the corded throat and tight shoulders to the feet planted squarely on the dry ground.

Teri came up beside him. 'He doesn't know, does he?' she asked, very quietly.

'What would have been the point?' came the harsh response.

So quickly that she caught him off guard, Teri looked up into Rafe's face. She thought she had never seen so much pain in a man's eyes.

Without thinking about what she was doing, she put her hand on his arm. 'No point,' she agreed through sudden tears.

'He couldn't have done anything to help.'

'But maybe I can help, now that I'm here.'

'You?' Rafe withdrew his arm from her hand. 'What can you do, Teri? You're only a visitor.'

'That's not fair.'

'Fair,' he mocked roughly. 'Who's talking fair?'

'You don't know that I *can't* help, Rafe.'

He laughed, a harsh, cruel, tearing kind of sound. 'This conversation is insane,' he said then. 'Come along, Teri. Time to get back.'

Rafe turned the jeep in the direction of the camp. They had driven no more than a mile or two when a turn-off Teri remembered caught her eye.

'Can we detour, please, Rafe?'

'There's not much point.'

'There used to be a pond there.'

'Forget it, Teri. Just forget it.'

'I realise it must have changed, but I'd like to see it again all the same. It was such a lovely place.'

'If I were you, I'd remember it as it was.'

'I want to see it.'

Rafe shrugged, and for a moment Teri thought he would ignore her request. Then he reversed the jeep a few yards before steering it into the turn-off. A little way down a bumpy, unused track he put on the brakes.

Teri stiffened with horror as she stared out of the window. Where once there had been a tranquil piece of water, with lily-pads floating on the surface and rushes all around, now there was only a barren depression ridged with eroded sand. There was not a drop of water here to show that the pond had ever existed.

Suddenly Teri put her hands in front of her eyes, and she was weeping. Without a word Rafe took the jeep out of the turn-off. Then he stopped the vehicle, and put his arm around the sobbing girl.

'It's all right,' he soothed. It's all right.'

She stopped crying at length. 'I'm an idiot, I'm sorry.'

'You're not an idiot.'

'I should have been prepared. It's not as if you didn't try to warn me. It's just so cruel.'

He stroked her hair. 'It's a shock, seeing it like this for the first time.'

His arm around her shoulder felt so *good*.

After a while she said tentatively, 'There really were other times when you comforted me, Rafe.'

'I know there were.'

'Do you remember the monkeys that stole my doll?'

He laughed against her hair. 'How could I forget?'

'And the cake that fell in the fire?'

'After you'd gone to such lengths to decorate it for your mother's birthday.'

Very softly, she said, 'Then you must remember the last time as well.'

The hand in her hair abruptly stopped its stroking, and the arm around her shoulder stiffened.

Teri pressed on regardless. 'Yesterday, you insisted you'd forgotten.'

'Don't push me, Teri.'

'I don't believe you've forgotten.'

'Can't you leave it?'

'I know you remember comforting me when we were leaving Lelaanie.'

'Don't, Teri.'

'And kissing me. I know you remember.'

'All right,' he said, his voice steel-hard now. 'I remember.'

'I knew it!'

'I remember all of it. How could I possibly forget? Holding you. Kissing you. Keeping myself under an iron control because you were so young, even if you did have the body of a woman. Wishing with all my heart that you were two years older and that I could ask you to stay at Lelaanie when your parents left. But I also remember something else.'

'What?'

'You made a promise, Teri.'

'Yes,' she said on a dry throat.

'You said you'd come back. You were going to visit Lelaanie as soon as you finished school.'

'I'm here, Rafe.'

'Why did it take you so long?'

'I wasn't quite seventeen when we left, for heaven's sake.'

'Do you think I don't know that? But eight years! I believe you could have come back, if only for a visit—if you had really wanted to.'

It was very hard for Teri to keep the promise she'd made to her mother. But she knew she could not break it.

'The fact is, I'm here. Why does it bug you so, Rafe, that it's now, rather than earlier?'

'It's the timing,' he said grimly.

'You seem to think that I schemed my moment to come back. That it was all calculated.'

'Wasn't it?'

'No, damn you, it wasn't!'

He made no answer to that, and when she twisted round to look at him she saw that his eyes were cynical.

'You're quite determined to hate me,' she said in a low voice.

'I told you yesterday that I don't hate you, Teri. I despise what you've done, but I don't hate you. I've never hated you.' Without warning, he pulled her into his arms. And then he was kissing her. Searing kisses, nothing like the hard, angry kisses of yesterday. Kisses of lips and tongue that explored her face, the contours of her cheeks and eyes. One earlobe then the other, with the soft skin catching between his teeth. The little hollow at the base of her throat. And then her throat itself, with his tongue sweeping up and down it in long, hard strokes that were so sensuous that Teri felt as if she were being driven to the very edges of sanity.

All at once he was pushing her backwards against the seat, so that she was lying on the leather, and his body was over hers. His mouth was on hers now, covering it, demanding a response with the urgency of his lips, and receiving it. There was nothing soft in his kisses. Just a hard, hungry passion, kindling such a response in Teri that a fire began to burn in her loins as she kissed him back, kiss for kiss.

Suddenly he made a sound in his throat and tore his mouth from hers. Then he was drawing himself up, and pulling her up with him, so that they were both sitting again.

'Rafe?' She looked at him uncomprehendingly.

'Go back home,' he said hoarsely.

'Rafe! What are you saying?'

'Go back to America.'

'No!'

'This isn't for us.'

I love you. The words were on her lips, but she bit them back. Instead she strove for composure. 'Why not?'

'Forget this ever happened.'

'But it did happen, Rafe.' She was trying very hard not to cry again.

'It shouldn't have. I was determined it wouldn't,' he said fiercely.

'Rafe...'

'Forget it happened,' he said again, roughly. And then he jerked the vehicle into gear, and exceeded the speed limit all the way back to camp.

In the days that followed, Teri stayed determinedly away from Rafe. Which was not all that difficult, for he seemed equally eager to avoid her. When he did have to speak to her, he was never actually unfriendly, but his tone would be impersonal, and his words to the point.

Teri spent as much time as she could with her grandfather. He enjoyed telling her about the past. About his exploits. About Beth, and about Tom when he was a little boy.

But after a short time Stuart Masters would grow tired. Sometimes his eyes would close while Teri was talking to him. And then she would be thrust upon her own resources.

And so she was glad when three of her relatives made their appearance at Lelaanie. Lyle, Bruce and Amy Stanton were the children of Beth's late brother, Edward. As such, they were about the same age as Teri's mother.

'Well, hi!' Teri ran gladly to their car, eager to greet them. 'What a lovely surprise.'

'Hello, Teri. Heard you were here.' Lyle, in the driver's seat, eyed her distantly. Bruce and Amy, when they got out of the car, were no more friendly.

Feeling a little hurt, Teri took a step backwards. 'Aren't you at all glad to see me? It's so long since I was at Lelaanie.'

'And how clever of you to return when you did,' Amy said, with a glance at her brothers.

Talk about shades of her meeting with Rafe! In light of their attitude, it was not surprising when the Stantons showed no interest in spending time with Teri. They were only interested in visiting Stuart Masters.

'I'm beginning to feel like a pariah,' Teri said to Rafe, on one of the very rare occasions when they happened to exchange a few words.

Rafe laughed. 'You're no worse than they are.'

'Are you going to explain what you mean by that?'

'I don't think that's necessary, do you?' was the mocking rejoinder.

Friendlier by far was the next visitor to Lelaanie. Alec Marlow had been Lelaanie's legal adviser as far back as Teri could remember. After spending several hours with

Stuart Masters, he had time for Teri. They sat together in the shade of a scarlet flame tree, and the lawyer sipped a cold beer while he asked Teri about her mother and her life in America.

Inevitably, however, there were days when she felt lonely. More and more frequently, her grandfather dozed off while they were talking, and spent the rest of the afternoon sleeping.

And so Teri began to drive out with the guests. Not in place of a guide, but with him. Increasingly she was getting back her feel for the miles of Lelaanie bushveld, so that much of the time she too could sense where they would see game.

The jeep was returning to camp one afternoon when Teri glimpsed a tiny animal huddling in the bush.

'Joshua! Please stop.'

The guide drew the vehicle to a halt, then looked at her enquiringly.

'A baby impala, Joshua.'

'Yes, a baby.'

'I don't see its mother.'

The little scrap of an animal looked totally forlorn. Even from a distance Teri could see it was trembling.

'Maybe a lion...' The guide left the sentence unfinished.

'Oh, but that's terrible. The poor little thing. What about the rest of the herd?'

'Maybe it got left behind.'

'That would be it.'

Joshua was looking at his watch. 'Be dark soon. Best be moving on.'

'Yes,' Teri said. 'I guess we do have to go.'

Though she said nothing more about the impala all the way back to camp, she could not get it off her mind.

Poor motherless scrap. What possible chance did it have of surviving?

She went in to see her grandfather and spent a few minutes telling him about her day. About the little impala she said nothing.

There was still some light when she came out of the rondavel. In a flash she made her decision. Her grandfather had said she could use his car whenever she wanted; she had the keys to it on a hook in her bedroom. Taking a piece of canvas from one of the sheds, she went quickly to the car, and without a word to anyone she drove out of the camp gates.

She remembered almost exactly where the jeep had stopped. And there it was, the little impala, just as they had left it. A tiny bundle, huddled in the bush. With night coming fast, there was no time to lose.

In a moment Teri had left the car and was running across the dry veld grass. The baby impala, all big liquid dark eyes, looked at her nervously as she approached, but it did not try to run away.

Putting her arms around it, Teri felt the tiny body shivering violently against her own. She tried to lift the impala, but it was not a puppy that you could just pick up with one hand. It was all long, straggly legs, and lifting it proved surprisingly difficult.

Still, somehow she managed. 'I'm not going to hurt you,' she was soothing gently, when her arm was grabbed savagely.

Teri gasped with shock, and her heart thudded painfully in her throat.

'What...?' she got out, jerking up her head.

'Idiot! Crazy idiot!'

Six feet two inches of very angry man towered menacingly over her.

CHAPTER FOUR

'YOU'RE hurting me.' Teri tried to struggle out of Rafe's grip.

'Not a fraction as much as a lion would be hurting you right now if it had got to you first.'

'Let me go, Rafe!'

'When you're back in the car. Not before.'

'Will you help me carry the baby impala?'

'March! And be quick about it.'

'I'm not leaving without it,' she said.

'Come on, Teri!'

'Not without the impala,' Teri resisted.

'You stubborn little fool.'

'Rafe, the impala's been orphaned.'

'Perhaps...'

'It won't last the night in the bush if we don't rescue it. Aren't you going to help me?'

Rafe looked down at her, his expression one of sheer exasperation. Surprisingly, though, there was something else in his eyes as well. Something Teri had not seen since she'd come back to Lelaanie. But this was not the time to analyse what it was.

A moment passed, and then he bent, lifted the impala out of her arms, and carried it easily to the jeep.

Teri followed him. For the first time she was aware of the deceptive loneliness of the twilight veld. The great masses of bush where lions or leopards could be hiding, and you would never know they were there. The lengthening shadows over the dry grass, heralding the darkness which would soon make driving hazardous on unlit game-park roads. The chill that hung on the air.

She shivered, glad all at once that Rafe, however furious—and she knew she had not heard the last of his fury—was with her.

He insisted on settling the impala in his jeep. Then he walked Teri to her car, and waited while she got in and closed the door.

'Drive slowly,' he ordered.

'I always do.'

'Slower than usual. A lot slower. Didn't you notice how dark it's become? It's too easy not to see animals in this light. I don't want you running over anything.'

'I'll be very careful,' she promised.

'Then get going now.'

'I'll wait till you get in the jeep.'

'That's not necessary,' he said curtly.

She shot him a grin. 'You could be eaten by a lion too, you know, Rafe.'

Her provocation earned her a steely look. Then he shrugged and made for the jeep. There was something so totally confident in his manner that Teri realised that, even if Rafe had thought she was heading for trouble, he had no doubt about his own ability to look after himself.

Twenty minutes later they were back in the camp compound. Teri parked her grandfather's car in its carport. By the time she had jumped out and made for the jeep, which had come to a stop a few yards further on, Rafe already had the door open.

'Let me take it,' she said, when he'd lifted out the impala.

'It's all yours.' He put the shivering little animal into her arms. 'And now that you have it, Teri, what do you plan to do with it?'

She looked at him. 'The barn?'

'That would be the best place. There's some fresh straw in there.'

'I guess I'll be needing some milk.'

'And a feeding-bottle.' Quite unexpectedly he was smiling down at her. 'I should think Betty would be able to help you with that. Camp cooks keep the oddest things on hand at all times.'

'Yes, well. . .' His attitude was unsettling at a moment when she had expected anger. 'I'll just settle this little animal, and then I'll see what Betty can give me.'

The next half-hour was a busy one. Teri made a little enclosure around the straw in the barn. When she had settled the impala she went to the kitchen and, as Rafe had anticipated, Betty knew right away where to find a baby's feeding-bottle. Teri warmed some milk, filled the bottle and carried it back to the barn.

Huddled in one corner of the enclosure, the little impala was still shivering. Putting her arms around it once more, Teri cuddled it till it was a bit calmer. Then she held the bottle to the animal's mouth, and to her great relief it drank.

'This is a sight to behold,' a familiar voice said.

Teri looked up. 'I didn't hear you come.'

'Straw muffles sound. How is your baby, Teri?'

'Settling down. Poor little Annie, she must have had quite an ordeal.'

'Annie?' Rafe was laughing. 'You've named her, Teri?'

'Of course.'

He was still laughing as he dropped on to the straw beside her. 'Let's put her back in the enclosure now.'

'In a moment. I enjoy holding her.'

'No, she's calm now, Teri. Here, let me take her.'

With his long arms, it was easy for Rafe just to bend over the impromptu walls of the enclosure and to put the little impala on the bed of fresh straw.

Then he turned back to Teri. 'Will you leave her now?'

She wondered if he would laugh at her. 'I was planning on spending the night here, Rafe.'

But he was not laughing. 'I thought you might, so I brought you something.'

'Oh?'

'Coffee and some toast.'

She was touched. 'That's something I didn't expect. Thanks, Rafe.'

'Two and a quarter spoons of sugar in the coffee.' She heard the smile in his voice. 'And there's cream cheese and cinnamon on the toast.'

For a moment Teri was silent with astonishment.

Then she said, 'It's incredible—so many years, and you actually remembered.'

'There are some things,' Rafe said, 'that are hard to forget.'

She peered up at him, trying without much success to see his face in the dimness of the barn.

'Does this mean you're not mad at me any more for rescuing Annie?'

'I'm still mad, Teri.' But the hateful anger was missing from his voice.

'Rafe...'

'Sit back,' he said, 'and drink your coffee while it's hot.'

There was only the wall for support, and that was hard and cold.

As if he'd read her thoughts, Rafe put his arm around her, coaxing her to lean back against him. 'You may as well be comfortable.'

For a few minutes there was just the sheer joy of Rafe's body so close to hers. Teri closed her eyes, and wished she could stay in the circle of his arms forever.

Then he spoke. 'What made you do it?'

'Rescue Annie? I had to. I guess you think it was stupid.'

'It *was* stupid, Teri, no matter how good or kind your motives were. How often did I tell you that wild animals are not pets? That you can't look out for each and every one of them?'

'An orphaned impala,' she said stubbornly. 'Just a few days old at most. It didn't have a hope of surviving on its own, Rafe.'

'You're probably right about that.'

'If you agree, why are you so mad?'

'Because of the way you went about things. Without saying a word to anyone.'

'I'm sorry, maybe I should have said something,' she conceded. 'By the way, how did you know where to look for me? It wasn't just coincidence that you came by when you did.'

'Joshua,' he said grimly. 'You were gone, and so was the car, and it was getting dark. Joshua found me looking for you—he didn't know you were gone until then, or he'd have been after you like a shot himself—and it occurred to him that you might have gone back for the impala.'

'Oh...'

'It was a damn fool thing to do, Teri. There could have been lions. A leopard maybe, or a cheetah.'

'I had a feeling there weren't.'

'You couldn't know. Lions can hide in a few inches of grass.'

'You're lecturing to me, Rafe.'

'You bet I am!'

'I was just thinking of the impala.'

'An impala, yes. But what about your grandfather, Teri? What would it have done to him, do you think, if you had been attacked? And then there's...' He stopped. She felt his arm tighten fractionally around her shoulder, but he didn't go on with what he was saying.

'I'll be more careful next time,' she said slowly.

Again she felt the tightening of his arm. 'There must be no next time. If you need to walk into the bush for any reason whatever, come to me first. And if I'm not around, find one of the guides. Promise me that, Teri.'

More promises.

'OK,' she said.

They were quiet for a while after that. From the straw in the enclosure came the small snuffling noises of the impala. It was moving around, settling itself.

Teri sat with Rafe's arm around her, sipping her coffee and eating her toast.

It was Rafe who broke the silence at length. 'You still take forever to drink your coffee.' He sounded amused. 'A sip every minute or so. It must take you an age to finish a cup.'

'It's the way I enjoy it,' she said contentedly.

'You sipped in just that way when you were sixteen.'

So he remembered that too, did he?

But what she was enjoying far more than the coffee was the feel of Rafe's body all around her. The strength of his arm around her shoulders, and the hardness of his chest against her back. The maleness of the smell that filled her nostrils. Since Teri thought it unlikely that there would ever be another man for her than Rafe, this time with him was sheer bliss.

He laughed suddenly, and she looked up at him.

'Sitting with you here like this brings back other times, Teri.'

'Really?' she asked softly.

'You were always one to look after little lost things. Remember the little giraffe?'

'And the water buck... Both orphaned, too.'

'And the monkey, Teri? Skippy the monkey?'

'Skippy,' she said delightedly. 'Sure, I remember Skippy! After all our kindness, he rewarded me by throwing my favourite blouse over the fence, where it got all snarled up on a thorn bush.' She looked at Rafe, though she couldn't really see his face. 'Our memories go back a long way.'

'If only you hadn't had to leave.' He said it against her hair.

'I keep telling you—I've come back.'

'Temporarily only.' His voice had hardened, destroying some of the mood.

Determined to recapture it, Teri said, 'Those other times—when we sat up together—do you remember what we talked about?'

'Yes...'

'We'd tell each other about our dreams and plans for the future.'

'Your dreams at the time were never of a big city and a career-girl life, Teri.'

'But your dream was always of the bush,' she said, refusing to be baited.

'Yes.'

'You'd tell me how you came to be a game warden.'

'You still remember it, Teri?' he asked softly.

'Will you tell it to me again?'

'I don't think so.' His voice was suddenly harder.

'Please, Rafe. It's so long since I heard it.'

'You'll go back to San Francisco, and you'll tell your friends about the ramblings of some unsophisticated bushveld hick.'

'I would never do that. Besides, you're neither unsophisticated nor a hick. Rafe, please.'

And so he began to tell her about the farm in the Cape where he had grown up. His parents had been cattle farmers, and for years Rafe, the oldest of three brothers, had taken it for granted that he would be a farmer too.

'You always loved animals, Rafe. You used to collect stray dogs and cats and birds. You blame me for rescuing Annie, but there wasn't a lost or injured animal that didn't find refuge with you.'

'Hey,' he laughed. 'Who's telling this story? You or me?'

'You.'

He told her about the year his father was ill, and how he'd been responsible for the running of the farm at the tender age of eleven. And he told her about the vet he had worked for during one particular summer holiday, and the thoughts he'd had of perhaps becoming a vet himself.

'And then, when I was fourteen,' Rafe said, 'my Uncle Mike invited me to spend a week with him in the Kruger National Park.'

'Your Uncle Mike was a game warden.'

'You *are* doing the telling.'

'No,' Teri said. She knew this story almost as well as if she'd last heard it yesterday, and not eight years ago. But she loved the low vibrancy of Rafe's voice, the cadences, the way his words made his breath fan across her cheek. 'I want to hear you tell it. I won't interrupt you again.'

'That week changed my life. The idea that a huge tract of land, thousands upon thousands of acres of land, had been set aside for the preservation of wild animals, fascinated me. I watched Uncle Mike at work, I went everywhere with him. I was up before dawn each day, I was determined not to miss a minute of what he did. And by the end of that week I knew that I had to be a game warden.'

'Which wasn't easy to accomplish,' Teri said.

'For a boy who'd lived all his life quite a distance from the Kruger Park—no, it wasn't easy. But somehow I managed. I became a game warden. One thing led to another. And eventually I ended up leaving the Kruger Park, and coming to Lelaanie. I was just nineteen.'

With the telling of this story, Rafe had become once more the man Teri remembered. There was not a trace of the hateful sarcasm, the insinuations to which she had been subjected from the moment of her arrival.

Not that Teri expected this mellow mood to last. Whatever it was that bothered Rafe about her had not vanished. Tomorrow the animosity might be back and the daggers drawn once more. But at least tonight was different. Tonight was special. She wanted to remember tonight.

'I was eleven,' she said. 'I still remember the day you arrived, Rafe.'

He laughed softly. 'I remember it too. You were a skinny slip of a girl with pigtails and the biggest green eyes I'd ever seen. I knew even then that you would be beautiful one day.'

She looked up at him, and despite the darkness their eyes seem to lock. Teri wondered if Rafe knew that she had loved him even then. A different kind of love. The worshipful, adoring love of a very young girl.

Leaning her head against his shoulder, she asked, 'Have you ever regretted leaving the Kruger Park for Lelaanie?'

'Never. I learned more from your grandfather than I ever learned from any other man. Except perhaps my father.'

'When did you become Grandpa's partner, Rafe? That's the part that happened after we left. The part I know nothing about.'

'Five years ago. The day I was finally able to acquire a half-share of Lelaanie was one of the proudest of my life.'

'I can imagine. It was the day you fulfilled a dream.'

After a moment, Rafe said, 'Part of a dream.'

Teri was caught by something odd in his tone. '*Part* of a dream?'

'There was something else I wanted too...'

She tensed. 'What?'

'It doesn't matter any more,' he said flatly. 'It can never happen now, anyway.'

They grew silent after that, as if suddenly there was nothing more left to say. Teri got to her feet and looked into the enclosure.

'I wonder if I should be giving Annie some more milk.'

'She's quiet, Teri. Leave her be.'

'OK.'

'Are you sure you want to stay in the barn all night?'

'Of course.'

'In that case, I'll fetch us something warm.'

Her heart raced. '*Us*, Rafe?'

A big hand touched her face, pushed a strand of tangled hair behind her ear, then moved in a stroking movement down her cheek to the corners of her lips.

'Did you think I'd leave you here alone, Teri?'

With that, he got up and left the barn. He was back soon with a rug and two pillows.

'Snug?' he asked, when he'd covered her.

'As a bug,' she laughed.

'Good. Because I'm coming in with you.'

Without so much as a by your leave, he edged in beside her. And then he put his arm around her once more and drew her head back against his shoulder. As if it belonged there, Teri thought.

Turning her towards him, he kissed her, quite lightly.

'Goodnight,' he said then. 'Try and sleep, Teri.'

He must have been tired, because he fell asleep quickly. Remembering that he'd left camp at daybreak, Teri could not blame him. As for Teri, with the beat of Rafe's heart against her throat, and the roughness of his sweater against her cheek, it was hours before she slept.

It was the smell of the coffee which woke her. The faintest grey light illuminated the barn.

'Sleepyhead,' said a vibrant voice, as Teri opened her eyes.

Rafe, an alert-looking Rafe, freshly shaved and showered, was laughing down at her. 'Here's something to wake you up. And I've brought a bottle of warm milk as well. Your Annie looks decidedly hungry to me.'

Sitting up, she took the steaming mug he held out to her. 'Thanks. You look as if you're ready to face the day.'

'I am. I'm just off. Good luck with Annie.'

'Thanks. Was I very selfish, Rafe?'

'Selfish? In what way?'

'Letting you stay in the barn with me all night when I should have remembered you'd have to leave for work at the crack of dawn.'

Kneeling down beside her, Rafe ran his fingers through her tangled hair. 'Actually—it was worth it.'

'Really?'

'You've changed so much, Teri. It's much more than just your clothes and your accent and the words you use. More than the fact that your coming here at this particular time is very strange. I hardly recognise you.'

'I see,' she said dully, wondering what the long night had been all about.

'And yet yesterday...'

She looked at him. 'Yesterday?'

'You showed me that there was at least one side of you which hasn't changed at all. Where the animals are concerned, you are still the kind, caring, impulsive Teri I used to know. I like that.'

Rafe was hovering by the camp gates one afternoon as Teri arrived in one of the jeeps. He waited till the guide and all the camp guests had dispersed, then he said, 'Teri...'

'Yes, Rafe?'

And then she saw his ashen face, and the smudges beneath his red-rimmed eyes. In a second she was trembling.

'Something's happened to my grandfather!'

'It was very sudden.' His voice shook.

'Oh, dear heaven!' Her hand flew to her mouth. 'I should have been here. With him...'

'You couldn't have known. Nobody was expecting it. Not just then, anyway.'

'Oh, Rafe.' Her eyes were full of tears now, and her body was shaking. 'I came all this way to be with him, but I wasn't here when he needed me.'

'You couldn't have known,' he said again.

His arms went around her, and they held each other in a moment of silent grief.

But the moment could not last. Stepping away from her, Rafe said, 'There are things to be done.'

There were phone calls and arrangements to make. Teri phoned her mother. Rafe made all the other necessary calls, including those to the Stantons and Alec Marlow.

Stuart Masters was buried beside his beloved Beth in a secluded piece of ground near the camp. Only the people who knew him best were present: his guides and game wardens and all the rest of the camp staff, Rafe and Teri, Mr Marlow and the Stantons, a few cronies from other game parks, who left immediately after the funeral so that they could drive back along the unlit roads before dark.

Later, Alec Marlow assembled all those remaining to read the will. It did not take him long to deal with the first bequests. Not one member of Lelaanie's staff had been forgotten; all of them received generous bequests. Each of the Stantons was left some money as well. Rafe Mathias, 'whom I could not have loved more had he been another son', received Stuart's treasured writings and photographs.

Clearing his throat, the lawyer looked around him, from Teri to Rafe, to the Stantons.

'I now come to the major bequest, the remaining money, and the deceased's half-share of Lelaanie. All of it goes to his beloved granddaughter, Teri Elizabeth Masters.'

A stifled gasp of shock left Teri's lips, and her body went rigid. Involuntarily she looked at Rafe. He had been watching her, she realised with a further sense of shock. His eyebrows lifted fractionally in acknowledgement. Beneath them his eyes were cynical and unsurprised.

They were all watching her now, the Stantons with undisguised hostility, Alex Marlow with thoughtful speculation. And Rafe. Of them all, only the lawyer looked as if he was well disposed towards Teri.

There was an absolute hush in the room. It was so quiet that Teri was convinced that the wild beating of her heart must be heard by all. The rigidity of her body lasted only a few seconds as it gave way to a trembling that made her feel weak.

Looking from one to the other, she finally understood the reason for all the animosity she had encountered since coming to Lelaanie. From the start, Rafe and the Stantons had seen her as a threat.

What they did not know was that she had had no idea of her grandfather's wishes, just as she had no intention of accepting the bequest. She opened her mouth to tell them so, but her throat was so tight all at once, her lips so dry, that she was unable to speak.

As she reached for a glass of water, she saw the lawyer shake his head at her in an infinitesimal movement. In Teri's fevered state, the wordless warning meant nothing to her.

She had put the glass down and was about to say her piece when Amy Stanton chose the moment to break the silence with a vicious shriek. 'Gold-digger! You planned to come here when you knew your grandfather was dying. You manipulated him into changing his will.'

'Please, Miss Stanton!' the lawyer interposed harshly.

But Amy would not be silenced. 'We were to inherit Lelaanie—my brothers and I. It was only when this…this schemer…arrived, that the old man changed his mind.'

'That was his right,' Alec Marlow said.

'We'll contest the will,' Lyle declared. 'If Uncle Stuart had been in his right mind, he would never have left Lelaanie to Teri. Not after the despicable way her father just took off and abandoned him. It's quite clear our poor uncle no longer knew what he was doing.'

It was at that particular moment that Teri changed her mind about refusing the bequest.

'Stuart knew exactly what he was doing.' Rafe spoke for the first time. 'Stuart Masters was the most intelligent man I ever knew. And he was lucid to the end.'

Again there was silence in the room.

'That's your opinion,' Bruce Stanton said then.

'It's my opinion, too,' said the lawyer.

'Lyle's right. We'll contest the will.' This from Amy. 'We won't let the gold-digger get away with it.'

'You may contest, of course. That is your privilege.' Alec Marlow's voice was coolly professional. 'However, I think it only fair to tell you that it may cost you a great deal of money, and it will benefit you nothing in the end. Stuart Masters knew exactly what he was doing.'

'Which I shall testify to in court,' Rafe put in.

Teri looked at him in surprise. Rafe coming to her aid was indeed an unexpected development.

It was obvious Amy thought so, too. 'You know as well as we do, Rafe, that Teri wouldn't have inherited if she hadn't come to Lelaanie when she did.'

'That is pure speculation on your part, Miss Stanton,' the lawyer answered for Rafe. 'The fact is that Teri is her grandfather's beneficiary in the last will he ever made. That's as much as need concern us.' Gathering up his papers, he got to his feet. 'This concludes my part in the proceedings. If you'll excuse me...'

Teri, who had not uttered a word since the moment the will had been read, followed him out.

'Teri, my dear.'

'Mr Marlow—may I speak to you?'

He smiled at her. 'Certainly. In my rondavel, I think. Whatever it is you wish to say, we'll have privacy there.'

It was pleasantly cool and quiet in the shaded, stone-floored rondavel. There was a small table by the window, a chair on either side.

'Now, Teri,' Alec Marlow said, when she was sitting opposite him.

Teri put a hand to an aching head. 'I have to tell you, I was on the point of refusing the bequest.'

'I know you were.' The lawyer smiled at her. 'Didn't you see me warning you not to?'

'Did you? I saw you shake your head. I didn't realise...'

'It would have been most unwise, Teri.'

'Would it?' She looked at him, and he saw that she was very pale. 'The Stantons are probably right, Mr Marlow. I believe Grandpa only changed his will because I was here.'

'Would it matter so much if he did?' The question was asked very gently.

'Well, yes. I mean, Amy and her brothers, they think I planned the trip deliberately. That I knew my grandfather didn't have long to live.'

'We both know that's nonsense.'

'It's what Rafe thinks, too.' Teri's voice shook.

'Ah...'

Teri looked at him thoughtfully. 'Are you saying you think I should accept the bequest?'

'It's what your grandfather wanted, Teri. We had a long talk. He bitterly regretted the break with your father, and through it the break with you. As for your coming here... You made his last weeks very happy. He loved you very dearly, Teri. It was very important to him that you should have his share of Lelaanie.'

'The Stantons might still decide to contest.'

'I don't believe it for a moment. All their screaming was just bluff. They know they haven't a chance of success.'

Teri looked out of the window and beyond the fence to where a heat-haze shimmered like a pool of shining water on a huge bare rock. Beyond that, and on all sides, was the bush. Acres and acres of bush. And animals. Thousands of animals, unseen, but there. All part of Lelaanie.

'It's hard to believe that it's really mine,' she said, turning to the lawyer with a smile.

'Yours and Rafe's. You each own half of it now.'

The smile left her face. 'Yes.'

She turned to the window again. This time she kept her eyes on the bush as she said, 'What will I do with Lelaanie, Mr Marlow?'

'That, my dear, is something only you can decide,' he answered her quietly. 'But there's one piece of advice I want you to heed. Don't make any hasty decisions. Think very carefully before you make up your mind. On anything.'

It was not till very early the next morning that Teri had a chance to speak to Rafe alone.

She found him at his jeep, dressed in heavy boots and denim overalls. His hair was still damp from his shower, and he looked so dynamically attractive that she felt her heart thudding hard inside her.

'I guess you're on your way out.'

His eyes glinted. 'Good guess.'

Very early each day he left the camp in his jeep with a crew of men. He was fresh and alert now, but when they returned at dusk, Rafe and the men would all be looking tired and grim. Teri would have given much to know where they went, but so far he had never told her.

'Can you spare me a moment, Rafe?'

'More than one. The others aren't due for another ten minutes.'

'It won't take that long. I...I just wanted to say thank you.'

'For what?'

'Standing up for me yesterday.'

His eyes were on her face. There was something so assessingly male in the look he gave her that for a moment she felt breathless.

'You don't have to thank me for that.'

'You didn't have to take my side. Especially if it's true that the Stantons were originally meant to inherit Lelaanie.'

'I don't hold a brief for any of those three.' Rafe's voice was hard. 'Parasites if ever I saw any. Greedy, lazy people, who don't know the meaning of work. Constantly sponging on your grandfather. Always playing on his sympathy. I'd have hated to have them as partners.'

'So that's why you stood up for me.' Something, some small unreasoning feeling of happiness, died inside her. 'A case of me rather than them.'

'It wasn't a case of you or them,' he said impatiently. 'I did it for your grandfather.'

'Oh...'

'They were insulting him, Teri, suggesting that he didn't know what he was about. I couldn't let them get away with that, don't you see?'

'Yes,' she said after a moment. 'I think I do.'

Teri looked away from Rafe. With her eyes on the veld, she said, 'I didn't know my grandfather was ill when I decided to come to Lelaanie.'

'Why are you telling me this?'

She turned back to him. And now she was looking at him steadily, her eyes holding his. 'I could never understand why you were always so sarcastic. So offhand... From the start I realised something was wrong, but I never realised what it was.'

'I see.'

'You kept asking why I didn't come sooner.'

'You've never given me an answer.'

There had never been a time when she was more tempted to break the promise she had made to her mother.

'It wasn't possible. That's as much as I can say.'

'So we're back to square one, Teri.'

'No! It always puzzled me why you kept on about my timing, Rafe. Of course, after last night I understand.'

'You sound so convincing.'

She decided to let that one pass. 'The timing seems suspect, I can see that now. But it was a coincidence, really it was. I wish you'd believe me.'

Without warning, he touched her face, letting his fingers trail down one cheek, lightly, so lightly. Teri had to force herself to stand very still in order to conceal the torrent of feeling rushing through her.

'It would be so easy to believe you. You have the face of an angel. So sweet and pure. So beautiful. Even more beautiful than when you left here eight years ago.'

She was burning from his touch. Not just her face, where his fingers lingered; it was a burning sensation that extended to every inch of her body.

'Why won't you believe me, then?'

His hand dropped to his side, and his eyes left her face. 'I can't, Teri, I'm sorry. I just feel there has to be more to all this than the coincidence of your deciding one day that it was time you paid a visit to Lelaanie.'

She decided to give it one last chance. 'Haven't you wondered how we would have got to hear about Grandpa? You never let us know he was ill. Nor did Alec.'

'News travels all the time,' he said brusquely, brushing that particular argument aside. 'The grapevine has always flourished. I don't know how exactly you got the news, I simply believe that you did.'

It was time to change the subject. 'So we'll be partners now,' she said.

'Partners. Yes.' There was such a strange expression in the eyes that swept over her once more. 'Can you and I be partners, Teri? What do you think?'

'*Business* partners.' The expression in his eyes, the tone of his voice, were unnerving. 'I don't see why not.' She tried to keep her voice steady. 'What do *you* think, Rafe?'

'I can't answer that yet, can I?'

'You did say you'd have hated to deal with the Stantons.'

'They'd have given me a hard time, those three. They'd have tried their best to order me around, and never done a stroke of work themselves. Not that I'd have let them get away with any nonsense.'

She tried throwing him a teasing look. 'How do you know things will be any different with me?'

But his tone was serious. 'It would have to be, wouldn't it? We'll have so little contact, Teri. You'll be living your life in America, I'll be taking care of things here.'

'Doesn't sound like much of a partnership,' she said thoughtfully.

'We'll have to work it out, I suppose. I'll keep you informed of anything major. There won't be much in the way of profits at first—things haven't been too good lately—but when we do start making some money, I'll find a way of sending you your share.'

'I see,' she said dully.

'You sound doubtful, Teri.'

'If I do, it's because it sounds all wrong somehow, Rafe. Owning a half-share of Lelaanie, yet living thousands of miles away.'

'There is that...'

And then Rafe said, 'Teri?'

She looked at him.

'What if...?'

But he stopped right there, for at that moment his crew came walking across the compound towards the jeep.

'What if?' she prompted.

'Forget I said that.' He grinned at her. 'At least for now.'

CHAPTER FIVE

THE STANTONS left early that same day. Some time during the previous evening they had apparently reached the conclusion that there was no point in contesting the will, and now they could not wait to sever all ties with Lelaanie.

Teri was at the car as they were leaving. Amy, Bruce and Lyle were the only relatives she had left in Africa, and she wanted very much to stay on good terms with them. But their undisguised hostility made the cordial words she had been about to speak die in her throat. Sadly she watched them drive away.

'Don't waste your time being miserable about those three,' a businesslike voice advised.

Teri turned to see Alec Marlow coming up behind her. 'This isn't the way I wanted things to be, Mr Marlow. I'd hoped we could remain friends.'

'Some things aren't meant to be. Those Stantons were always just out for themselves.'

She glanced at the travelling bag in his hand. 'You're not leaving too, are you? I thought perhaps you'd stay a while longer.'

'Have to get back home, I'm afraid. I've a big trial on tomorrow, and a mass of notes to read through before then.'

'Will you come again? Just for a visit?'

'I'd like that very much.' He smiled at her as he put out his hand. 'Good luck with Lelaanie, Teri.'

'I'll need it.'

'You'll do just fine. I've the same confidence in you that your grandfather had.'

He was in the car and about to drive away, when he rolled down his window and gave her his parting advice. 'Remember, Teri, no hasty decisions. Think carefully before making up your mind on anything.'

When the lawyer's car had vanished from sight, Teri made her way to the impala's enclosure. To her great satisfaction, Annie was thriving: enjoying her food and getting stronger and more confident every day.

Cuddling Annie, Teri wondered how she was going to spend her first day as co-owner of Lelaanie. In the event, she was not to wonder long. She was still at the enclosure when Joshua, one of the guides, appeared with the news that the other guide had not turned up for work that day.

'Is Amos ill?' Teri asked with quick concern.

'I do not know.'

Teri knew that many of the camp staff had their homes a little way out of the compound. 'Has anyone been to find out?'

Shifting his feet uneasily in the sand, Joshua did not meet her eyes.

'Who took the people out at dawn, Joshua?'

'I did. There were only six who wished to go.'

It happened quite frequently that not all the guests went out for the early-morning drive, some of them preferring to sleep in and wait until later. In that case one guide was enough for the first shift. But two guides were always needed later in the morning, when everyone at the camp joined the drive.

It took Teri just a moment to understand what she had to do. 'I'll take one of the jeeps.'

'It would be best.' Joshua looked relieved.

'Just as well I've had practice.' She smiled at the guide. 'I'm nowhere near as expert as you, Joshua, but I hope the guests will be happy with me.'

Chuck and Donna Baker, an American couple from New York, were less than happy. Their six-day stay at Lelaanie was just one part of a holiday in Africa to which they had been looking forward a long time, and they were determined that each day should be memorable. Cameras and binoculars slung around their necks, they were unable to conceal their disappointment as they stared at Teri.

'Surely the guide wouldn't just let you down at the last minute?' Chuck asked, his look, as he took in Teri's youthful appearance, being one of dismay.

'Amos is ill. I know he was sorry he couldn't be with you today,' Teri said, wishing that Joshua hadn't already departed with his share of the guests. They could have made a last-minute seating change.

'We were so hoping Amos would show us some lions.' This from Donna. 'We've yet to see a lion, you know.'

'Yes, well... Lions are a matter of luck most of the time.' Teri managed a smile. 'But I'll do my best to give you a good day.'

Chuck looked doubtful. 'Without meaning to offend you, little lady, what can you know about the African bush? You're as American as we are.'

'I grew up at Lelaanie, and some things you never forget.' This time Teri's smile came easily. 'I was born with a feeling for the bush.'

It was a feeling that surged to the fore in her that day. And luck was with her too, starting with two giraffe about a mile out of camp. A magnificent pair, their necks gracefully entwined as if in some kind of mating ritual.

It was a wonderful sight, one that was duly recorded by every camera in the vehicle.

A few miles further on Teri spotted a flash of movement deep in the bush. Her passengers were puzzled when she stopped the vehicle.

'Can you really see something?' Chuck asked, his tone suggesting she had stopped for nothing.

'Buffalo—I think.' Teri knew she was taking a chance on this one. At this point, what she had was little more than a hunch.

'Where?' asked one of the others.

'I'm going to edge up a bit. I've a feeling there might be more of a view further on.'

Slowly she took the jeep a few yards farther. And then a little further still.

And suddenly there they were! A herd of buffalo clearly visible through a break in the trees. Horns rounded and lethal, bodies solid and powerful, heads turned suspiciously in the direction of the vehicle.

'Wow! That's some animal!' Chuck breathed, clearly impressed. 'Is the African buffalo really as dangerous as they say, Teri?'

'Every bit as dangerous,' she told him smilingly. 'That's why I've kept the engine running. With buffalo, as with elephants, it's always best to be able to get away quickly if you need to. You never know when they'll get mad and decide to charge.'

But her mind moved from the buffalo as she waited while her passengers took their pictures and looked their fill. Chuck and Donna's earlier doubts still rankled a little.

A few days earlier one of the game rangers had mentioned seeing lions. On the road east, he'd said, near some big rocks. The road east was not popular with the guides, for it was nowhere near water and there was usually not much game to be seen along it. As for rocks, Teri was not sure where they were. And even if there were lions in the area, if they were lying in long grass— as lions have a habit of doing much of the day—there would be little chance of seeing them anyway.

Still, it was one more hunch worth following.

Lelaanie's guests were puzzled as she took the unfamiliar road east. Teri said nothing, but inside her an unpleasant feeling of apprehension was building. If she was wrong, her charges could be in for a less than interesting morning.

Her apprehension grew as she saw the high clump of bare cliff looming to the right of her. Long dry grass everywhere. There could be a pride of lions just yards from the road, and they would never see them.

The jeep had just crested a slope when Teri saw them. A whole family of lions in the middle of the road.

Two huge male lions, manes magnificent. Two smaller females. And four little cubs, tumbling over each other in playful frolic.

Excitement stopped the breath in Teri's throat as she managed to bring the jeep to an almost noiseless halt.

The happiness and excitement of her passengers knew no bounds. *This* was what they had all been waiting to see since the day they had made plans to go to Lelaanie.

'Lions!' they cried in one voice.

'Look at the darling cubs!'

'Those manes! Never seen anything like it!'

The lions took no notice of the jeep. Kings of the jungle, lords of the road. Theirs to decide when they would move aside for a mere vehicle to pass. But the vehicle had no intention of passing. The people inside it were ecstatic, happy to remain immobile for as long as the lions chose to remain in the road.

One of the male lions rose, lazily stretched, then walked up to the jeep and sniffed the petrol. A too-playful cub received a rebuking cuff from one of the females.

It was a scene straight out of a safari-lover's heaven.

The enchanted humans could have watched all day, but the lions tired of the road at length and made for the bush. Moments later they were out of sight.

Finding a spot to turn, Teri drove the jeep back in the direction of the camp. Instinctively she knew that to go on in the hope of finding other game could only make for an anticlimax.

It was quite late in the afternoon when Rafe and his crew of men returned to camp. The fires had already been lit around the fence, and Teri, who knew the golden rule about not driving on game-park roads after dark, had been getting concerned about Rafe's safety.

She was at the jeep, and about to talk to Rafe—a dusty, muddy, tired-looking Rafe—when Chuck appeared at her side.

'For you, Teri,' he said, as he thrust a bottle of champagne into her hands.

She was bewildered. 'Chuck, why?'

'For giving Donna and me the most exciting day we've had in years.'

Rafe said, 'I don't understand.'

'Amos was ill today and this little lady filled in for him. The lions she showed us have been the highlight of our trip.'

Rafe's eyes were on Teri's face. 'You'll have to tell me about it.'

'Yes, of course,' she said, when all she really wanted to do was to caress the tired lines from his face.

'You've got yourself quite a partner, Rafe,' Chuck told him. 'The lady's a trouper. Never imagined she had it in her.'

A glint came into Rafe's eyes. 'So she intrigues you too, does she?'

'Sure does! Hey, guys, Donna's waiting for me with the other bottle of bubbly. I'd best get back to her.'

Rafe smiled down at her when Chuck had gone. 'Sounds as if you had quite a day.'

'It's your day I want to hear about.'

The smile vanished from his eyes. 'Not the sort of day that makes for pleasant conversation, I'm afraid.'

'I want to hear about it, anyway. I want to know where you go every morning, you and the men. And why you come back so late, and looking so tired.'

'You're sounding a bit like a wife, did you know?'

She was glad that it was probably too dark for him to see the sudden warmth in her cheeks. 'I think I sound like a partner, Rafe. A *business* partner.'

'Now, listen, Teri . . .'

'With a right to know what's going on.'

He raked a hand through his dusty hair. 'I need a shower and some food. I'm really not in the mood right now for polite conversation.'

'I have a steak waiting to go on the braai. Why don't you take your shower while it's cooking?'

A wary look came into his face. 'This is something new.'

'I'm only inviting you to have supper with me, Rafe. Will you come?'

'Do you see this as a new pattern in our lives, Teri?'

The flush in her cheeks deepened, but she said hardily, 'Who said anything about a pattern? I just thought that since this is our first day as partners it might be a nice idea to have a meal together.'

He looked down at her. So tall and utterly male. So sexually attractive that, dust and all, she would have gone willingly into his arms. So silent.

'And if you have any thoughts of saying that you don't fancy my steak, I'll crown you, Rafe Mathias.'

To her relief he grinned. 'Now, why would I be so ungallant? I'm off to shower, Teri. I'm sure the steak will be delicious.'

The steak was succulently tender by the time Rafe joined Teri by the fire outside her rondavel. In their jackets of aluminium foil, the potatoes were nicely baked, and a tossed green salad was in a dark wooden salad dish.

Rafe lifted steak and potatoes from the fire, and put them on the plates Teri held ready for him.

'We're supposed to be drinking to your eventful day,' he said as he sat down. 'I don't even know what happened.'

'I don't feel like champagne, Rafe. Not tonight. Not so soon after Grandpa...'

'I'm glad you feel that way,' he agreed quietly. 'I've no taste for it either.'

'But if we were celebrating,' Teri said, 'I'd want to drink a toast to our partnership.'

Rafe's hand stopped in the act of cutting his steak.

Something tightened inside Teri. 'Is there something wrong with that?'

'Not really,' he said after a moment. 'Except that nothing's really settled.'

'That wouldn't affect what we might have been toasting.' Her smile hid an uneasiness within her.

Rafe did not answer that one. Instead he asked her again about her day, and what had made it so eventful.

'Good thinking,' he praised, when she told him about the lions.

'The Bakers thought so. In fact, they all did. You should have heard the clicking of camera shutters.'

Rafe laughed. 'That I believe.'

And then Teri said, 'I can't believe Grandpa's gone.'

'I can't either,' he said quietly.

'I keep thinking I'll look in on him after supper.'

'It does feel strange to know that Stuart's not at Lelaanie any more. I've been thinking about him all day.'

'You'll miss him, won't you, Rafe?'

'More than I can tell you. I revered Stuart Masters above any man I ever knew.'

'You were never afraid of him?'

'No. It's true that Stuart was a tough master. Hard and demanding. There were many who feared him. But he was intensely compassionate. And what some of those men didn't understand was that he never expected more of any person than he did of himself.'

'That's not quite true. He expected too much of my father,' Teri said quietly.

'Perhaps he did. I think he realised it himself—when it was too late—but your father never gave him a chance to say he was sorry.'

'Maybe not.'

For a while after that they were silent. A little way away the voices of the camp guests rose and fell. Somewhere in the distance a drum sounded, its beat throbbing and mysterious on the cool night air. Louder than all the other noises were the sounds of the bushveld: the ceaseless shrilling of the crickets, the barking that sounded so much like dogs, but which really belonged to baboons, the small high calls of unseen game.

Supper was finished and they were drinking their coffee when Teri brought up the subject that had never left her mind since she'd seen Rafe return with the jeep.

'Are you going to tell me where you go every day?'

As he put down his cup, she saw the way his lips tightened. 'Is it really necessary?'

'I'd like to know.'

He looked across at her, and now there was not a trace of lightness in his face. 'I have to warn you—it's not a pretty story.'

A tight knot was beginning to form in the pit of her stomach. 'I want to hear it all the same.'

'The drought. You've seen some of the devastation, Teri.'

'The day at the look-out point ... And there've been other times.'

'I told you there was more.' He paused a moment, then went on. 'Dry waterholes, Teri. Frantic animals trying to find water where there isn't any.'

'Is there something you can do?'

'Have you any idea what it's like, Teri?' His voice was taut with pain. 'Some of the animals are thirst-crazed. They use the last of their strength to dig for water beneath the sand. Sometimes they find a few drops, but it's never enough.'

'You told me you'd been putting down new boreholes.'

'Right. We have to provide other places for the animals to find water. And in some measure we're succeeding.'

'Some measure?' she repeated slowly.

'There are too many animals still going to the old places. They're creatures of habit, Teri. We have to move them. Physically.'

'And that's what you're busy doing every day? You and the men?'

'One dam in particular is only mud now. The animals get stuck in it.'

'And you rescue them?'

'We try. But it's a slow business. Back-breaking. Heart-breaking. And so terribly slow.'

'When will there be an end to it?'

'I don't know.' For the first time there was a hint of despair in his voice.

'I should be out there helping you.'

'Don't be silly.'

'We're partners, Rafe. We're in this together now.'

'That,' he said, 'is something else we should talk about.'

Picking up a long stick, he leaned forward in his chair and stirred the coals. They had let the flames die low, but now there was a bit of an orange flicker amid the dusty grey. Teri watched him tensely.

Then he sat back in his chair, and looked at her. 'I want to buy you out.'

She stared at him. 'Would you repeat that?'

'You heard me the first time. I'm offering to buy you out, Teri.'

'That's insane!'

'Not if you think about it properly.'

Feeling a little ill, Teri looked at him across the flickering flames. 'Is the thought of having me for a partner so abhorrent to you?'

'I didn't say that.'

'Then *why*?'

'It makes sense. What can Lelaanie mean to you, when you'll be thousands of miles away from it? Oh sure, I know I told you I'd let you know of any major happenings, and I would. Just as I'd make certain you received your share of the profits, if and when we start to start to make any.'

'But it's not the way you want things to be,' she said quietly.

'I can't see why you'd want it, either,' he countered, without actually answering her question. 'If Lelaanie really meant anything to you, you'd have returned years ago.'

'We're not back to that, are we, Rafe?'

'No, we're not. Enough's been said on that topic already.'

'Then why bring it up?'

'Merely to make a point.'

There was a dull feeling of pain in her chest. Rafe didn't want her here. That was what this was really all about.

'The point being what?' she asked, her voice low.

'That you'd be far better off being paid what your share is worth. That way you could go on living the good life, and forget that Lelaanie—and all that goes with it—ever existed.'

'It's not something I *could* forget, Rafe.'

'That's what you say now. And maybe you really think it. But a month back in San Francisco and you'll think otherwise. You'll be grateful then for my offer.'

After a long moment Teri said, 'You told me things aren't good financially at Lelaanie.'

'That's right, they're not. All the more reason why you'd be better off getting out.'

'But if things are really so bad, Rafe, I'm wondering how you're proposing to pay me.'

'You don't need to wonder about that.' His voice was hard. 'We'll get in an independent person to appraise the game park. You'll get your fair share, I promise.'

'That isn't my question.'

'You mean you're wondering if I have that much money? The answer is that I don't. Not in cash, anyway. But I'll get a bank loan. I'm almost certain I can get one. I'm well known in these parts, and my credit-standing is excellent. They'll be prepared to wait while I ride things out here at Lelaanie. Until I can repay the loan.'

'That could take years.'

Rafe shrugged. 'That would be my problem, Teri, not yours.'

'Still, I'm curious why you'd lay such a burden on yourself. Somehow I don't believe my grandfather would have expected it of you.'

Across the veld, just then, came the trumpeting of an elephant. The sound bounced off the kopjes and echoed through the camp compound. Teri waited till the last echo had died away before speaking again.

'Besides, Rafe, you're just taking it for granted that I'll be going back to America.'

He sounded surprised. 'Won't you?'

'I don't know. Alec Marlow warned me not to make any hasty decisions. Not to let myself be rushed into anything.'

'I'm not trying to rush you, Teri. You don't have to give me an answer tonight.'

'I couldn't, even if you wanted one. I need time, Rafe.'

'Take all the time you need.'

'I intend to.'

'But if you decide to sell to me, then we'll go ahead and get Lelaanie appraised.'

'And if not?' she asked.

'We'd have to come to a workable arrangement. One that would suit us both.'

'A workable arrangement.' The words had such a cold impersonal ring to them.

'I take it you wouldn't want to be in on all the everyday decisions, Teri. Just the major ones.'

'And I take it,' she countered, suddenly very angry, 'that you're just taking a darn sight too much for granted. For one thing, you're just assuming that I'm going back to America.'

'That's where your life is.' He sounded genuinely surprised by her anger.

'People do move around. In my case, I would only be returning to the place that was my home. Because I do look at Lelaanie as home, no matter how you happen to think I feel about it.'

'But your mother is in America,' he said slowly.

'What of it? When I was sixteen I had no option but to go where my parents went. I'm an adult now, and people do live in different places from their mothers. I love Mom dearly, but she is married to a very nice man now. With Philip in her life, it won't matter if I'm not there as well.'

'And then,' Rafe said deliberately, 'there is Larry.'

Teri drew in a swift breath of astonishment. *'Larry?'*

'Your man.' His tone was totally devoid of expression.

'You're crazy,' she protested. 'Larry isn't my man. He's my boss.'

'A boss you call your darling?'

'Good grief! You must have listened to my phone call when I first arrived. Rafe, how could you?'

'It wasn't planned, I assure you. I just happened to walk into the office at that moment.'

'And stayed to listen. And you keep talking about me being unscrupulous,' she accused him indignantly.

'Do you make a habit of calling your boss your darling?' Evidently he was not at all put out by her anger.

'You only heard one side of the call.'

'Meaning?'

'If you'd heard both sides, you might have understood.'

'You said you were missing him.'

'I do miss him. And I'll miss him even more if I don't go back. Larry is a very nice man. Warm. Funny. A delight to work with.'

Rafe's lips tightened. 'Then it's obvious you must go back,' he said flatly.

Teri got to her feet. Without a word, she left Rafe and the warmth of the fire, and walked to the fence. A half-moon hung in the cloudless, star-studded sky, silvering the veld with its light. The bushes were indistinct humped shapes, merging one into the other. It could have been bushveld anywhere.

Except that this was game country. Teri did not have to see any animals to know they were there. Thousands of animals in the bush that was Lelaanie, and the game parks beyond it. Living the life of the jungle, the life of Africa since time immemorial.

Rafe came up behind her, his footsteps making no sound on the soft ground. He leaned his elbows on the fence, so close to her that his arm brushed against hers, and his thigh touched her hip. Teri could do nothing to stop the burning feeling that seemed to sear her whole body at the contact.

For two minutes at least they stood there together in the darkness, with the sounds of the veld in their ears and the smell that Teri would forever associate with Lelaanie in their nostrils. Even when the maniacal laugh of a hyena came from somewhere near them, they did not speak.

Suddenly a lion roared. A long, low, reverberating roar, sweeping the bush with its sound, seeming to silence every other sound with its fierceness. Thrilling, evocative, awesome.

Again it roared, and then again, kindling Teri's blood, exciting emotions that were already raw. Beside her she felt the slight tensing of Rafe's body. Even he, man of the outdoors, of the wild, accustomed to all the sounds of the bush, was stirred by this one sound that was like no other.

The lion roared once more. Then it was silent. And the veld, as if its lifeblood had stopped flowing during the time when the lion had asserted his domination, came alive again, the air ringing with the shrilling of the night insects, the distant drums beating out their song.

There were tears misting Teri's eyes, but she did not know if Rafe could see them as she lifted her head to look at him.

'That was an omen.'

He laughed softly. 'Another omen?'

'Yes.'

'What kind of omen this time, Teri?'

'Telling me what my decision must be.'

Beside her, the long body was suddenly taut. 'Oh?'

'I belong to the bushveld, Rafe. I'm part of it.'

'I think you're a bit over-excited.'

'No! This is my home, Rafe. My real home.'

'You don't know what you're saying.'

'I do! Something seemed wrong back there at the fire when we were talking. But now I know. I'm certain.'

'Teri...'

'I'm staying at Lelaanie, Rafe.'

'You're just feeling a bit emotional right now.'

'Darn right I am! Because I know that I'm doing the right thing. The *only* thing for me.'

'You said you weren't going to make any hasty decisions,' he said harshly.

'This isn't hasty. This is *right*. Every part of me says it's right. I'm not selling out, Rafe. Nor am I going back to America. I'm staying on at Lelaanie. You've got yourself a new partner. An active partner, Rafe.'

'You'll feel differently about it in the morning.'

'No way, Rafe. I believe this is what my grandfather wanted for me.'

'You don't know that, Teri. You don't know that by leaving you his share of Lelaanie, Stuart wasn't just giving you security.'

'I believe he wanted me to live here. To go on where he left off.'

'This is madness, Teri.'

'Then it's a kind of madness I happen to fancy.'

'You're a stubborn lady.' He sounded part rueful, part amused.

'Better believe it!'

'You've no idea what you're letting yourself in for. We've so many problems here at Lelaanie. You could go back to America and never have to worry about a thing.'

'If there are problems, we'll face them together,' she said confidently.

'Maybe.'

'I know it.'

In a different voice, Rafe asked, 'What about us, Teri?'

'*Us*, Rafe?'

'You and me. Alone together at Lelaanie.'

Her pulse began a sudden racing. 'I'm not frightened of you, Rafe, if that's what you're getting at.'

'Perhaps you should be. Because you know only too well what I'm getting at.'

'Rafe...'

'Yes, Teri. That spark between us. The insanity that seems to drive us both when we're together.'

'Is it insanity?' Her chin was lifted, her tone provocative.

'You know it is—and yet I can't seem to help myself.'

His hands went to her shoulders, gripping them. And then he was pulling her against him, and his kiss was hard and possessive, yet at the same time achingly sweet. Making her yearn for more. Much more.

But for once, Teri resisted him. Realising that Rafe was only trying to make a point with his kisses, she twisted her head away. 'No!'

'Why not?'

More than anything, she would have liked to make love with him. But not now, not in these circumstances, when she knew that Rafe was only trying to prove a point. This was not how she wanted it to be.

'I just don't want to,' she said shakily.

'Because you're thinking of Larry?'

Tears stung her eyes. 'I can't bear it when you talk like this. None of this has anything to do with Larry.'

'No?' She could tell he was not convinced.

'You don't know how I *hate* it when you're in this mood.' She pushed herself out of his arms. 'Why do you have to be so cruel, Rafe?'

For a few seconds he did not answer. When he did, he sounded a little less certain of himself. 'How are we going to handle ourselves, Teri?'

If he loved her as she knew she loved him, there would be no problem. The trouble was not just that he did not love her. He did not even trust her.

'We'll have to find a way of dealing with it, Rafe.' Deliberately, she stepped beyond his reach. 'Goodnight—partner,' she said softly.

And, before he could make anything of that, she turned and left him.

Dawn was just breaking the next day when Teri realised that there was a new problem at Lelaanie. The early-morning coffee and hot chocolate, with which the guests normally warmed themselves before going out in the jeep, had not been made. Betty, the camp cook, was missing from the camp.

'I'll see to it,' said a sleepy-eyed Teri when Rafe stopped at her rondavel to talk to her.

'I doubt there will be breakfast after the drive, either.'

His tone was so hard that she was suddenly alert. 'How do you know that Betty isn't just late this morning, Rafe?'

'Did you know that Betty is Amos's wife?'

'Yes, of course. How is Amos, by the way? Is he back at work today?'

'Afraid not.'

'No problem. I'll take the jeep out again today.'

'You don't mind?'

'Why should I? Actually, I'm delighted to be able to do something useful.'

'Hm,' was the only response, but the eyes that swept her flushed, sleepy face were thoughtful.

Teri had to force herself to remain calm under the intenseness of that look. 'Listen, Rafe, about Amos and Betty, do you think they could be ill with the same thing? I should go and see if I can do something for them.'

'I'd leave them alone if I were you.'

'But why? I mean, it could be something serious. We might have to get a doctor.'

'I doubt a doctor would be any help in this instance.'

'You're trying to tell me something.' She frowned up at him. 'Are you saying they're not ill at all?'

'Exactly.'

'Then where are they?' But all at once she understood without him having to tell her. 'Have they left Lelaanie?'

'If my guess is correct.'

'Without a word to you? To either of us?'

He nodded.

'It's so hard to believe. They've both been here so long. Why would they suddenly leave?'

Rafe just stood there, hands shoved into the pockets of his jeans, looking down at her.

'Because my grandfather is no longer here?' Teri asked at last.

'I would say that's it.' Rafe hesitated. 'You may as well know—two of the men who've been working with me at the dam have left as well.'

'I don't understand it, Rafe. What's happening here all of a sudden?'

'Your grandfather made very generous provision for all his staff. There's enough money for them not to work if they don't want to.'

'I know that. But still... I mean, this is so sudden, these people have all been here for years. They all know you, Rafe. They respect you.'

'Yes...'

And then Teri really did understand. 'It's *me*. That's it, isn't it, Rafe?'

'It could be,' he conceded. To his credit, he did not seem happy making the admission. 'But it's nothing personal against you, Teri, you have to understand that.'

'Then what is it?'

'I'm sure you remember that African tribal customs are very strong in this part of the world.'

'I do remember,' she said slowly.

'The men we're talking of are quite old, and they all belong to the same tribe. They've been at Lelaanie many years, most of them, and it goes against their pride and their tradition to be employed by a woman. It's something they've never been exposed to.'

'What about Betty?'

'I'd say she is probably just following her husband's wishes.'

'But I wouldn't have been bossy, Rafe. I respect the men far too much to give them any orders. I know that they understand the bush much better than I ever shall, and I'd never throw my weight around.'

'I know that. But tradition is a hard thing to fight, Teri.'

'What do we do now?'

He grinned at her. 'That's quite a question coming from a gutsy lady like you.'

A lovely warm feeling began to spread right through her at his smile. 'You mean I refuse to give up?'

'That sounds more like the Teri I'm beginning to know again.'

'You're right!' She smiled back at him. 'I'm not scared of hard work, Rafe. I'm very fond of Amos and Betty and the others, and I hope they'll be back. But if not...'

'We'll have to look for new people,' he finished for her.

'Younger people perhaps, who will be willing to work in a place where there's a woman.'

'That's it. But it doesn't solve today's problem, Teri. At the risk of sounding like a chauvinist myself—did you really mean it about making us all hot chocolate and coffee? I'd do it myself, but I should be leaving for the dam.'

'Of course I meant it!' Teri said. 'It's really no big deal, you know. Give me five minutes to get dressed, and I'll be there.'

CHAPTER SIX

THE DAYS that followed were busy ones. Starting with the early-morning kitchen duties, it went on from there. Rafe had put out the word that Lelaanie was in need of a cook and a new guide, but so far none had been found. Joshua would drive the one jeep, Teri the other. And, although she never achieved a repeat performance of the lions and their cubs, the guests were usually highly entertained with what she did manage to show them.

After the early-morning drive it was back to the camp compound, and while her charges went to their rondavels to exchange warm clothes for shorts and T-shirts Teri went directly to the kitchen and began to prepare breakfast. Half an hour later the guests would sit down to a meal of eggs and bacon, and the pancakes which Teri had learnt to make in America.

'Where is Rafe?' asked one of the guests one morning.

'In the bush with the men.'

'Seems to spend all his time there. Spotted him leaving at the crack of dawn.'

'Yes.'

'Comes back just before dark, I notice. Is there really so much to do here?'

All morning Teri's mind had been with Rafe and the men at the drying dam. It was more than a week since he had told her what they did there, and every day she wondered how they were getting on, and if they were safe.

But she said with a lightness that hid her concern, 'Oh, there's always lots to do at Lelaanie.'

After breakfast the guests usually spent about an hour in the camp compound, reading, resting, or standing at the fence with their binoculars before going out in the jeep again to search for game.

Teri looked at her watch. Ten in the morning. It would be early evening in San Francisco; a good time to make her calls.

'Teri! Are you OK?'

The last time Teri had spoken to her mother was to let her know about her grandfather's death. That call had been difficult. This one would be too, though in a different way, which was probably why she had delayed making it until now.

'We're missing you. Have you booked your flight home?'

Teri gripped the telephone tightly. 'There's something I have to tell you. Grandpa left me his share of Lelaanie.'

A startled exclamation came through the line from half way across the world. 'Why didn't you say anything last time we talked?'

'I didn't know then. Only after the funeral, when Alec Marlow read the will. And then...' She took a breath. 'I had a lot of thinking to do.'

'When are you coming back, Teri?' There was a note of urgency in her mother's voice.

'I'm not. Actually—I've decided to stay.'

'No!'

'I want this to be my home. Mom, please understand. Please, please understand.'

'Oh, Teri...' There was a sob in her mother's voice.

And then Philip spoke. 'I'm on the other phone, and I managed to catch some of that. This has come as a shock to your mother, Teri, but I know she wants you to do what you have to. I'll take care of her.'

Dear, strong, understanding Philip. Her mother would be in good hands.

'Do you feel I'm letting you both down, Philip?'

'Of course not, Teri. Neither does your mother. It's your life, and it's obvious you love Lelaanie.'

'Oh, I do. So much.'

'Then go for it. And when we've saved a bit of money, your mother and I; we'll be out to visit you.'

'I'll hold you to it.'

'You do that.'

And then her mother was speaking again. 'Take care, darling. Good luck with Lelaanie. And remember that we both love you.'

There were tears in Teri's eyes as she put down the phone. Though there was no doubt in her mind that she had made the right decision, she loved her mother and Philip as much as they loved her, and she knew that she would miss them.

Only when she felt that she had herself sufficiently under control did she make the next call.

'You're out of your mind,' was Larry's flattering response to her news.

She was even able to manage a laugh. 'I hope not.'

'Burying yourself in the wilds of Africa.'

'I don't feel as if I'm burying myself. Listen, Larry, I feel terrible about giving you notice like this. Especially when you've been so good about keeping my job open for me.'

'So you should,' he said, but cheerfully.

'I'm sure you'll have no trouble finding someone to take my place.'

'I'm not so sure. But listen, Teri, you'll never believe this. There's a chance I may be going to Africa myself.'

'*Really?*'

'Remember the YZ Productions assignment?'

'The game parks of Southern Africa?'

'Got it. Anyway, seems Archie Logan has gone down with some kind of tropical bug.'

'Oh, no, poor Archie,' commiserated Teri, who had met and liked the cheerful producer.

'He's heading back home. And guess who they want in his place?'

'*You*, Larry?'

'None other. I'm just waiting for the final word, then I'll be flying out.'

'Larry, that's wonderful! The kind of opportunity you've always wanted.'

'You can say that again! Just keep your fingers crossed that it happens. And don't be surprised if the next time you speak to me it will be locally.'

Rafe and the men were always late coming back from the dam, but today they were later than ever. Teri was not surprised to see their muddy boots and overalls, their dusty and unsmiling faces.

Rafe said no more than a cursory 'hello' before walking away in the direction of his rondavel. But Teri was not hurt, nor did she press him for more. Her heart went out to Rafe and the others, for she could see that they were exhausted.

Camp dinners usually took the form of a braai. Teri supervised the lighting of the fires, and, with Betty gone, she saw to it that the meat and salad ingredients and parboiled mealies wrapped in foil were put out on big platters. As for the rest, she knew she could safely leave the guests to look after themselves.

Half an hour after Rafe's return to camp, she made her way to his rondavel.

'Come in,' came a muffled call in response to her knock.

'Rafe?' she asked tentatively, as she opened the door and found herself in an empty living-room.

'Oh, it's you, Teri. Through here,' she heard him say.

She put what she'd brought with her on the table, then went in the direction of his voice.

He was in the bedroom, stretched out on the bed, unclothed except for a pair of white shorts, his hands clasped behind his head on the pillow.

Heart beating suddenly faster, Teri looked at him from the doorway. 'I hope you don't mind...'

'Why should I? As long as you don't expect me to be good company.'

'Of course not.' She felt a little shy of him now that she was here. 'I thought you'd probably have showered by now.'

He laughed, the sound low and virile. 'As it happens, I have. But it's just as well you waited to visit me. You'd hardly have liked my company after almost twelve hours spent dragging animals from the mud.'

'Yuk,' she said, pretending to grimace.

'What brings you here, Teri?' He had not moved from his position on the bed.

'I thought you'd be thirsty. Hungry. I know it's been an exceptionally long day.'

'I'm not in the mood to join you for a braai tonight.'

'I didn't think you would be. That's why I brought some food to you here.'

He looked surprised. 'You did?'

She smiled at him. 'Remember the night we brought Annie back to Lelaanie? You brought me coffee and toast. This time it's my turn.'

It took her just a moment to retrieve her basket from the living-room.

'I knew you'd want a cold beer,' she said as she came back into the bedroom.

'You read minds! How on earth did you know I was lying here, trying to summon up the energy to go out and get one for myself?'

She was laughing as she went up to the bed. 'Didn't know I had telepathic powers, did you?' she teased.

He was laughing too. 'Truly amazing. What else do you have in that magic basket of yours?'

'Sandwiches and some fruit. I didn't know if you'd be up to anything more right now.'

'Wise woman. But you'll have to stay and share it all with me.'

She hesitated at that. Looking down at him, she felt an ache of desire stirring inside her. Six feet two inches of muscled male, unclothed except for those white shorts which only heightened the effect of his tan, there was something overwhelmingly sexual about him. No desk-bound man could ever look quite like this. There was virility in every inch of Rafe's superb body.

'Sit down,' he invited.

She looked around her. 'There isn't a chair. I'll go and get one from the other room.'

But he was patting the space beside him on the bed. 'There's room enough here.'

Her throat was suddenly dry. 'I don't think...'

'I told you, Teri, I've had my shower.'

The sparkle in dark eyes decided her. 'OK, then,' she said, and sat down on the edge of the bed.

He laughed at the sight of her feet positioned decorously on the floor. 'Not like that. Do you know how uncomfortable you look? Put your legs on the bed.'

She did as he suggested, and swung her legs up, so that she was lying back beside him.

And then she remembered his reaction the last time there had been any closeness between them. 'Are you sure this is a good idea?'

'You wouldn't ask that if you knew how exhausted I am. I'm almost too tired to open that beer. Besides which, we've had other meals in close quarters, Teri.'

Rafe put the plate of food next to him on the bedside table. Then he opened the beer and held the can out to her, motioning to her to have a sip. Teri, who had never been much of a beer lover, shook her head.

'The sandwiches look good. You'll have to help me with those,' he insisted.

Not realising quite what that would involve, Teri leaned across him. As the warm, bare skin of his stomach touched the underside of her arm, she felt suddenly dizzy. She was not sure if Rafe tensed, but for one startled moment her eyes met dark ones glinting in a shock of their own just inches from hers. Unsteadily, she retreated to her side of the bed.

For a few minutes they were both silent. Rafe sipped his beer. Teri ate her sandwich very slowly. She was in no hurry to repeat the experience of having to reach across Rafe.

But perhaps he had been unnerved by it too, for when she eventually finished the sandwich he passed the plate to her so that she could help herself to more. Her appetite had vanished, but she forced herself to take a few grapes. At least the act of eating gave her something to do.

Talking would be a help, too. 'I spoke to my mother today,' she told him.

'How did she react to your decision?'

'I think she's in shock,' Teri said unhappily.

'I can imagine.'

'Philip will take care of her, though. He's the kindest man you can imagine. He even spoke of coming to visit Lelaanie some day.'

'You'd like that.'

'Yes, I would.' She hesitated a moment, before going on. 'I also spoke to Larry.'

'Oh?'

'I had to tell him I'd decided to stay at Lelaanie, so that he wouldn't go on keeping my job for me.'

'I see.'

'He had some rather amazing news. It seems he's waiting for confirmation of a flight to Africa.'

'Amazing?' Rafe drawled. 'Obviously he misses you, Teri, and wants to see you.'

'It's nothing like that. He'll be working on a film. He'll be really busy all the time.'

'I should think he'll find a way of getting to see you, all the same.'

'Actually, I doubt there will be much more than a phone call or two,' she said quite calmly, wondering why Rafe should sound as if he cared. It was hardly as if he had any personal interest in her himself.

They talked of other things after that. Rafe wanted to know about her day; he seemed quite impressed by the fact that she was able to handle all the duties of the absent camp staff on her own. And then it was his turn to tell her about his own day, and she listened quietly while he talked.

Presently he put the beer can and the near-empty plate on the table beside him.

Teri felt suddenly shy once more. 'I guess I'd better be going.'

'Why the hurry?' he asked lazily.

'Well, you've finished eating. And . . . there are things to do.'

'Nothing that can't wait.'

Then he turned on to his side, one long strong leg bending over hers, and gathered her to him.

'I didn't think this would be a good idea,' she said bumpily.

Rafe cupped her chin in one of his big hands and ran his tongue along her throat. 'Can you think of a better idea right now?' he murmured against her lips.

And in fact her protest was already too late, for he was kissing her even as he spoke. Light kisses at first, yet so tantalising that they were almost unbearably sensuous. Kisses that made desire run like fire in her veins. And then the mood of the kisses changed, becoming hungrier, more passionate, as Rafe possessively staked a claim which Teri had never been in a mood to deny him.

All rational thought deserting her, she opened her mouth willingly to his, giving a little moan of pleasure as his body moved on the bed to cover hers. She was wearing shorts and a sleeveless blouse, and where her legs and arms were bare the contact with his warm skin was intoxicating.

'I thought you were exhausted,' she said, when they drew apart for a moment.

'I thought so, too.' He raised himself on one elbow and looked down at her. His eyes were deep and unreadable. 'It seems that I keep underestimating your effect on me.'

Her heart was beating in her throat. 'Rafe?'

'There are times,' he said roughly, 'when you drive me out of my mind.'

Joy pulsed in her veins. 'Really?'

'Hadn't you noticed?' he groaned.

He bent towards her again, and a sigh of pleasure shuddered through her as he slid a hand beneath the waistband of her blouse and began to caress the soft, bare skin of her stomach. He was kissing her again as he undid the front opening of her bra, and his hand cupped the fullness of her breast, capturing first the one nipple, then the other, caressing them, letting them harden against the roughened hardness of his fingers. And Teri, responding to his caresses with ones of her own, thought she would faint with the sheer joy of what he was doing to her.

There had never been any other man for her than Rafe. Rafe was the reason she had never allowed herself to fall in love during all those years in America. There never would be any other man in her life, kissing her, caressing her, as he was doing now. And, because she loved him, she wanted to give him as much pleasure as he was giving her.

Lifting himself away from her at length, he looked down at her again.

'You are beautiful,' he groaned.

'Am I?' she whispered.

'Beautiful. Sexy. The most desirable woman in the whole world.'

'*Really*, Rafe?'

'Really.' There was the strangest note in his voice when he went on. 'That's the problem.'

'I don't know what you mean.'

'Don't you, Teri?'

Without warning, he got up from the bed and walked over to the window, where he stood with his back to her.

'Rafe, what is it?' she whispered, her eyes on his rigid back and shoulders.

'I get too excited when I'm with you.'

'What are you saying?'

'And afterwards I blame myself for letting my emotions get the better of me.'

Her throat was dry. 'We've done nothing wrong.'

'It's no good, Teri.' His voice was grim.

'You started this!' she threw at him disbelievingly.

He spun round. 'Do you think I don't know that?'

There was torment in his eyes, but Teri was far too distressed to wonder what it meant.

'You started it,' she said again. 'I simply can't believe this is happening.'

'The only one I blame is myself.' His voice was subdued.

'I was the one who said it wasn't a good idea to begin with, and still you got me to lie beside you.'

'You were right, Teri. I'm so sorry.'

'Sorry? This is one hell of a time to tell me that,' she shot out furiously. 'Here I am on your bed, half-naked and feeling like an idiot, and you have the utter nerve to say that you're sorry!'

'The trouble is that I let my feelings drive me when I'm with you, Teri.'

She tugged at her blouse, shoving it abruptly back into her shorts as he watched her from the window.

His expression was bleak. 'I know you're angry. If it's any consolation, I'm even angrier with myself.'

'It's no consolation at all! I just wish I knew what this was all about, but I don't.'

'This isn't for us, Teri. That's why this whole partnership thing is going to be so darned difficult. It's what I tried to tell you the other night—we're fire and fire, Teri.'

'There's nothing wrong with that.'

'There is—because we're wrong for each other.'

'No, Rafe, it's all because you don't trust me. That's what this is all about.'

'That's not quite true.'

'It's been true since the day I came back.'

After a long moment he said, 'I can't let myself get close to you again, Teri.'

She stared at him. 'Why not?'

'I think you'll leave Lelaanie again.'

'And I don't know how to convince you otherwise.'

'It doesn't make sense that you could stay here permanently.'

'I keep telling you that I'll stay. Why won't you believe me?'

'It's not that I don't believe you, Teri. I think you really do mean what you say—for the moment. You're all enthusiastic about staying because everything is so new and exciting. Coming back here after all these years. The idea of owning Lelaanie. But you won't stay. Everything is against it.'

'I had to leave Lelaanie the first time. I didn't have a choice. I wasn't quite seventeen, for heaven's sake. I had to go where my parents went. And don't start telling me again that I could have returned earlier.'

'I won't. But it doesn't alter the fact that I'm convinced you will leave again. And this time it will be your own choice.'

'I won't, I tell you.'

'We're in for some tough times here, Teri. We have such problems at Lelaanie.'

'You're not telling me something I don't know. And I'm not frightened, Rafe.'

'No. You're not, are you?' His eyes were on her face, and she wondered what he saw there. 'You're not frightened. But you might get fed up. And when you do, San Francisco could seem like a mighty sweet place to return to.'

She forced herself to look at him, even though it hurt. 'You're so certain of that, aren't you?'

'Only because that's where your life is now. In America. True, you're enamoured with Lelaanie right now. But the time will come when you will hate the sameness, the primitiveness, and then you'll begin to hate it here.'

'You're so wrong.'

'You'll get bored, Teri. Restless. You'll miss the shopping and the night-life.'

'You really don't know the first thing about it,' she said angrily.

'And then,' Rafe said in a new strange voice, 'there's Larry.'

'I worked for him, Rafe.'

'You did say you'd miss your job.'

She swung her feet over the side of the bed and stood up.

'I remember saying it. It was an interesting job, and I enjoyed it a lot. It doesn't mean I'm going back.'

'You might feel differently about it when you see Larry again.'

'I told you—I doubt that will happen.'

'A sophisticated man from your own world, with everything to offer you. You'll realise what you're missing.'

'You don't know what you're saying.'

'Was Larry only your boss, Teri?' Again that strange note in his voice.

'What is that supposed to mean?'

'It seems very strange that he's taking this particular moment to come to this part of the world.'

'It's not strange at all. He's filling in for someone else. That's all there is to it.'

'Did you go out with him?'

'Now and then.'

'Did you kiss him, too? The way you kiss me?' he asked, very softly.

She came towards him with her hand lifted. In that moment she wasn't thinking. All she wanted was to hurt him, as he was hurting her.

But he caught her hand in his. His face was taut. 'Don't try that, Teri.'

'Then don't you dare try and make me out to be some kind of slut.'

'*Did* you kiss him, Teri?' His fingers were still around her hand, his grip hard.

Blindly, driven by the need to hurt him back, she said, 'If I did—and it's something you'll never know—it really isn't any of your damn business.'

'Teri . . .'

'You were engaged once, Rafe. I haven't asked you anything about that.'

'What would you like to know?' he asked, politely.

'Nothing,' she said. Which was a lie—there was a lot she wanted to know. 'Let go of my hand.'

Dark eyes glinted in the gaunt face, but his fingers released their pressure.

Without another word, Teri wheeled and made for the door. She did not turn back and look at the man by the window. If she had, the depth of pain in his face might have stopped her.

Teri had been co-owner of Lelaanie for a few weeks when the Moolmans arrived. She was in the office when Ed Moolman came in to register.

'Mr Moolman!' Teri welcomed him with a warm smile and an outstretched hand. 'It's great to see you.'

The tall, white-haired man in his early sixties stared at her in astonished recognition. 'It can't be...'

'Yes, I'm Teri. Teri Masters.'

'Well, I never! Teri Masters. All grown up and back at Lelaanie. This is a surprise.'

'Where is Mrs Moolman?'

'Wandering around the camp compound somewhere. Just wait till she sees you.'

Beatrix Moolman was as astonished—and as delighted—as her husband when she met Teri. Her face, a little lined after more than sixty years of outdoor living, spread into a pleased smile.

'You've come back, Teri. After all these years!'

'Yes, I'm back. It's wonderful to see you, Mrs Moolman.'

'And you. We were so sad, Ed and I, coming to Lelaanie with Stuart Masters no longer here. We almost didn't... How long have you been here, Teri.'

'Just a few months.'

'Are you here to stay?'

'My grandfather left me his share of Lelaanie.'

'This really *is* news,' Ed said.

'Is your mother with you?' Beatrix wanted to know.

'No. Mom's remarried, and her life is in America now. For a while I thought mine was, too. But ... Well, things changed.'

'They did indeed,' said Mrs Moolman. 'Teri, I look at you, and I can't believe how the time has gone. You were a little girl when we first began coming here. Not much older than my grandchildren are now.'

'Do you still come for a month every year?'

'We talk about it from one year to the next.' Ed smiled at her. 'Are you very busy, Teri? I hope you'll be able to spend some time with us.'

'As much time as you'll let me.'

For Teri, the Moolmans' visit could not have come at a better time. They were a warm, friendly couple, and she had always liked them, as had her grandfather, who used to look forward to their company.

As a youth, it had been Ed Moolman's dream to become a game warden. Thwarted in that ambition by his father, who had pressured him to enter his building construction business instead, Ed had compensated by spending at least four weeks of every year in the bush. It had been his good fortune that Beatrix enjoyed safari life as much as he did.

With the familiar presence of the Moolmans at Lelaanie, the tension which had existed between Teri and Rafe since the evening in Rafe's rondavel was somewhat dissipated. They had been too much alone together—together yet separate, for they had taken to avoiding each other as much as possible. Which was a difficult thing to do given the inevitable limitations of game-park life.

Most of Lelaanie's guests remained relative strangers, very few of them staying more than four or five days. Ed and Beatrix Moolman were friends. They would invite

Teri and Rafe round to join them for an after-supper glass of wine and a chat. And in the relaxed atmosphere of the Moolman rondavel the conversation would become general.

Rafe was able to talk about some of the problems that beset Lelaanie, the dreadful toll taken by the drought, the drop in guest occupancy, and the shortage of staff. Teri had engaged a new cook, and there was also a new trainee guide, but the game park still needed more men to help in the bush. There were times when Teri sensed that, although Rafe was addressing Ed and Beatrix, he was really talking to Teri herself.

After they had said goodnight to the Moolmans one evening, Rafe stopped her. 'How would you like to go for a drive with me tomorrow?'

Astonished, Teri lifted her head to look at him. It was too dark to see his face, but she decided that he sounded friendly enough.

'Is there a reason?'

'Something I'd like to show you.'

'What is it, Rafe?'

'A surprise.'

There was a smile in his voice. Although Teri had made up her mind not to let him affect her again, she could not help being intrigued.

'I can never resist surprises.'

'Three tomorrow afternoon?'

'Three is perfect for me, but you're never back from the dam by then.'

'If you say you'll come, Teri, I'll make it my business to be back.'

CHAPTER SEVEN

'ARE you going to tell me where we're going?'

Rafe turned his eyes from the road. 'It's a surprise. Remember?'

'I didn't realise it was *still* a surprise.'

'It is,' he said, with the smile Teri had not seen since the evening in his bedroom.

It was lovely to see the smile that warmed his eyes, for though Teri had made every effort to carry on normally since the afternoon in Rafe's rondavel the days since then had been quite a strain.

She was intrigued when he turned the jeep off the road and drove it into the bush, the heavy-duty wheels moving easily between the trees and over the uneven underbrush.

'I never leave the road myself,' she said.

'I should jolly well hope not,' came the cheerful rejoinder. 'You know the rules.'

'Yet you seem to think the rules can be broken, Rafe.'

'They can be—by me.'

Again he was smiling, and Teri understood that he was just teasing her.

Quite suddenly they emerged from the trees and into a clearing. And then Teri caught her breath. A few yards away was a family of giraffe. Two adults, very tall, very stately. Two tiny giraffe, moving unsteadily on legs that even now showed the promise of length. In its way, it was as exciting a sight as the family of lions had been.

Rafe switched off the engine, then turned to Teri. 'Well?'

'They're gorgeous, Rafe! Absolutely gorgeous.'

'I thought you'd like them.' There was a note of quiet satisfaction in his tone.

'I adore them! How old are they?'

'A few days.'

'A few days. And already they're walking. It's incredible.'

He was amused. 'They're not human babies, Teri.'

'I know. Just look at those wobbly legs. Aren't they something? How I wish I could take some photos.'

'Abracadabra,' Rafe said, and reached behind him.

'My camera!' Teri gasped in astonishment as he held it out to her.

'As you see.'

'But where on earth did you find it? I could have sworn I left it in my rondavel.'

'You did.'

'You mean... You don't mean you actually went in when I wasn't there and took it?'

He laughed. 'Exactly.'

'Rafe Mathias! Don't you have any scruples?'

'Aren't you glad to have your camera?'

'Ecstatic. But you haven't answered my question.'

'You answered it yourself, Teri.' And in a softer tone he added, 'I guessed you'd want it.'

When he was in this mood, it was impossible to be angry with him. Teri opened the camera case, and focused on the baby giraffe. Only when she had all the photos she wanted did she turn to Rafe once more.

She found him watching her. There was such an odd expression in his eyes that for a moment she felt totally unnerved.

'Why did you bring me here?' she asked at length.

'I thought this was something you'd want to see.'

'You went to so much trouble, Rafe. You left your work at the dam early just for this.'

After a moment he said, 'That's true, I did.'

'Why did you bring me? The *real* reason.'

Very quietly, he said, 'A peace offering.'

Her throat was dry suddenly. 'Is that what it is?'

'My way of apologising. I behaved like a swine the last time we were together.'

Teri was trying very hard to control a sudden trembling. There were things she wanted to say, to ask, but she kept silent, sensing that Rafe had not finished.

'You had every right to be angry that day, Teri. I started the whole thing. I got you to lie on the bed with me, and then I humiliated you. My only excuse is that it was not what I'd intended.'

'I'd done nothing wrong,' she said in a low voice.

'No. In fact, you'd been very thoughtful, bringing me food when you realised I would be too tired to get it for myself.' Unexpectedly he put his arm around her shoulders. 'It's not your fault that you're so very sexy and beautiful. You can't help being the way you are. Just as you can't help the fact that I long to have you in my bed every time I see you.'

The words hit her, shaking her to the very core of her being, yet making her very happy at the same time.

But his next words were a bit of a blow. 'It's up to me to learn not to give in to my feelings.'

'You don't have to answer this if you don't want to, but Rafe...have you been hurt?' she asked quietly.

A moment passed. At length he said, 'Yes, I suppose you could say I've been hurt.'

By whom? The woman to whom he had been engaged? Teri waited a moment, but he did not elaborate, and she realised that she really did not want to hear the story.

'And you think I'd hurt you, too?'

'Yes,' he admitted honestly. 'You're so lovely, Teri. It would be so easy to let myself...' He stopped. 'To let myself get too used to having you around,' he finished then, but Teri had the oddest feeling that those were not the words he'd started to say.

'Rafe...'

'I don't want that to happen, Teri.'

'Because you still can't accept that I had no ulterior motive in coming here? And because you still don't believe that I'm at Lelaanie to stay?'

'I'm sorry,' he said, and he sounded genuinely regretful.

'One day you'll believe me.'

'Perhaps.'

'I'm determined you will.'

She leaned her head back. His arm was still around her, and he was sitting so close to her that his thigh lightly touched hers, and his breath was warm on her cheek.

'I would like us to be friends again, Teri,' he said after a little while.

'I'd like that, too.'

'I'm glad. I was anxious to make it up with you before I leave.'

She lifted startled eyes. 'You're going away?'

'There are some things that need doing in connection with Stuart's estate. Alec and the accountant want to see me; I won't bore you with the details. Which reminds me, I'll need some signatures from you.'

'When are you going?'

'Day after tomorrow. I'll be gone about a week. Do you think you can cope alone here, Teri?'

'Yes, of course. Don't worry about me. I'll just carry on as usual.'

'Chuck Baker was right about one thing, you're quite a woman.'

Rafe kissed her hair, and for a moment his arm seemed to tighten around her.

Then, with what seemed like an effort, he lifted his arm from Teri's shoulder, and put his hands on the steering-wheel.

'Time we got back,' he said.

Teri missed Rafe very much, but there was so much for her to do at Lelaanie that she did not have time to brood. And, at the times when she might have been lonely, she had the company of the Moolmans.

Ed and Beatrix were having a wonderful time. This was the holiday they looked forward to from one year to the next, and they made the most of it. They were up before dawn most mornings so that they could be ready to go out with the first jeep, but later, when the second trip was made, they often chose to stay in the camp compound, just relaxing.

Ed would read one of the many books he had brought with him, while Beatrix sat with her knitting. It seemed to Teri that there was never a time when Beatrix was not knitting a garment for one of her grandchildren.

Ed often teased his wife for being a doting grandmother. But his teasing never deterred her from producing the little albums she carried wherever she went, and showing off the photos of her eight grandchildren.

'Janey's a doll. Three years old, and already with such a mind of her own.' Beatrix looked fondly at the photo of her youngest grandchild.

Teri smiled. 'She sure is cute. They all are.'

'Yes, they are. Of course, every grandmother thinks hers are the most special grandchildren in the world.'

'Thank goodness for grannies. You must miss them very much, Mrs Moolman.'

'Oh, I do. Much as I'm enjoying myself, I can't wait to get back to them.'

'I bet.'

'Of course, we'll have to stop off somewhere first, Ed and I. Each child must have a present. Can't go back without things for the lot of them.'

'Do you know already what you'll buy?'

'No.' Beatrix was frowning. 'Souvenirs of some kind, if we can find them. That's what they all seem to want. They love souvenirs.'

'Where will you get them?'

'Ed will have to find a gift shop somewhere. One of those places that sells curios. Of course, it usually means going out of our way instead of going straight back home.'

'What a shame we don't have a gift store here at Lelaanie,' Teri said.

'It is a shame. It would certainly make things easier. I've often wondered why your grandfather never put one in. But there, I suppose he had his mind on other things.'

'I guess he did. And yet, you'd think a lot of our guests would want to take things back with them. Presents for family, mementoes for themselves.'

'I would think so,' Beatrix said.

She turned a page of the photo album, and went back to talking about her grandchildren. But Teri was no longer concentrating on what she was saying.

* * *

After breakfast the next morning Teri went in search of the Moolmans. She found them in their usual spot near the fence, Ed reading, Beatrix knitting.

Teri came straight to the point. 'I have a big favour to ask of you.'

Both Moolmans looked up, smiling. 'What is it?' Beatrix asked.

'This may be an awful nerve on my part—but do you think you could possibly cover me here for a couple of days? You wouldn't actually have to do anything. Martha, the new cook, takes good care of the kitchen. We have a new trainee guide, but there are so few guests here at the moment that Joshua can get them all into one jeep for the drives.'

'Why, yes,' said Ed, but they both looked puzzled. 'Are you going somewhere, Teri?'

'I thought I'd take my grandfather's car and drive into town.' She looked at Beatrix. 'Remember our conversation yesterday about the gift store, Mrs Moolman? Well, I stayed awake all night, thinking about it. We do need one.'

'Now, Bea,' Ed said reproachfully, 'you know better than to meddle.'

'No, Mr Moolman, I'm really glad it came up. I don't know why we don't have a gift store at Lelaanie, it certainly is long overdue. There are so many things we could stock here. Postcards. Books about the game parks and the animals. Carvings and jewellery made by craftsmen from around here.'

'My goodness, that does sound interesting,' said Beatrix enthusiastically.

'My mind is whirling with ideas. I can think of dozens of things we should have.'

'Don't you think that perhaps you should wait till Rafe gets back?' Ed asked cautiously.

'I'd rather not. I want to surprise him.'

'I don't know . . .'

'It's quite important to me.' For the first time, Teri hesitated. Then she said, 'Rafe has this idea that I'm not really serious about Lelaanie. That when the novelty of being here has worn off, I'll head back home to San Francisco.'

'You want to prove him wrong,' Beatrix said slowly.

'I must admit, it's partly that. But I really want to set up a gift store. The more I think about it, the more I realise how badly we need one. There's even the perfect place for it. Do you know the room next to the office?'

'Yes!'

'That's where I thought I'd locate it. At least for now. And while I'm in town, I'm going to do something about our low occupancy rates as well.'

'Do you have something planned, Teri?' Ed asked.

'I have an idea. Nothing more than an idea at the moment. But in my job back home in San Francisco I learned quite a bit about promotion. I want to see if I can put what I learned into effect here at Lelaanie.'

'This game park will never be the same again,' Beatrix said approvingly. 'Go along, Teri. Ed and I will be happy to see to things for you.'

'I don't know how to thank you.'

'You don't need to thank us, Teri. We love this place. Even if there were more people than Joshua could comfortably get into one jeep—and for your sake and Rafe's I wish there were—that wouldn't be a problem. Ed knows Lelaanie so well, and he's always longed to try his hand at guiding. He could accompany the trainee guide. Right, darling?'

'Right,' he said with a wide smile.

Teri left Lelaanie an hour later. By midday she was in town, and had booked herself into a hotel.

Larry Anderson would have been proud of his former employee, for she wasted no time in getting started. A telephone call to the co-ordinator of a local crafts club yielded immediate results, and Teri made an appointment to see Amanda Webster that very afternoon at the shop operated by the club.

She was immediately charmed by the quality and variety of the articles on display: Amanda's weavings, in glowing colours, wood etchings of trees and animals, batiks in warm autumn shades, lovely pottery, and hand-crafted jewellery set with the semi-precious stones found in the area.

Teri spent more than an hour walking around the shop, making notes and jotting down prices and the names of various craftspeople. Amanda walked by her side, answering her many questions.

At length, Teri turned to Amanda with a smile. 'I love what you have here. If I had my way, I'd take the lot, but unfortunately I have to be selective.'

Amanda looked pleased. 'I suppose you'll have to go slowly at first, and get a feel for what people want.'

'That's it.'

'Why don't you think about things for a few days? Then, as soon as you're ready, you can let me know what you want, and I'll tell our members to get busy.'

'I won't even take as long as that,' Teri assured her. 'I'll let you have my order by tomorrow morning.'

Her next stop was a little shop in which T-shirts took up most of one window. Some were plain, many had slogans or funny pictures printed on them.

The shop's owner was a young man with laughing eyes and a mop of red hair, who grinned when Teri asked him where he had his T-shirts made up.

'I do them myself.'

'You do?' She was intrigued. 'Do you think you could make some up for me?'

'Sure thing,' he said, when Teri told him that she wanted plain-coloured T-shirts with the picture of a lion's head printed above Lelaanie's name in bold letters. Small, medium and large, six T-shirts in each size.

'When can I have them?' she asked.

'Tomorrow afternoon soon enough?'

'Wonderful!' Teri gave the young man such a wide smile of delight that he decided she was the prettiest girl he had ever seen.

It was getting so late now that Teri knew there was little more that she could do in town that afternoon. Not that she minded, for there was so much that she had to think about before the next day.

The hours flew by as she sat in her hotel room and made her calculations. The gift store must have enough variety to make it attractive, yet, with Lelaanie's occupancy so much lower than it should be, there were not enough guests at the game park to support anything too ambitious.

Next morning Teri waited impatiently for the shops to open. After placing her orders and making all her purchases, she took a large flat folder from the car and set out to visit the travel agencies as well as some of the bigger shops. To her great satisfaction, most of them were agreeable to displaying the promotional poster she had designed.

Early the following day she returned to Lelaanie, the boot of her car filled with all the things she had bought.

She could hardly wait to see Rafe's face when he saw what she had accomplished.

Teri was smiling to herself as she sat down at her dressing-table and began to brush her hair.

It was sunset. Soon it would be too dark to look across the fence into the veld. In the camp compound the fires had been lit, and the guests were sitting around sipping beer as they exchanged stories of the animals they had seen that day.

For Teri, it had been a good day too. Apart from the time she had spent in the jeep with the new trainee guide, she had worked many hours in the gift store. Already, after just a few days, the previously unused room was looking transformed, with gift items displayed on small tables, and batiks and wall-hangings and some bright posters on the freshly whitewashed walls.

'Care to tell me why you're looking so pleased with yourself?' asked a vibrant voice.

'Rafe!' Teri's eyes sparkled with pleasure as they settled on the man who had come up behind her, his reflection joining hers in the mirror. Then she spun round on the stool. 'I didn't even know you were back.'

His hands were on her bare shoulders, turning her, so that they were both looking at each other in the mirror once more. 'I brought you something.'

'What?' she asked, knowing that the only thing she wanted from Rafe was himself. And then, becoming suddenly aware that she only had on bra and panties, 'My goodness! I'd better get dressed.'

'You look wonderful just as you are,' he said huskily, and she saw his eyes on her breasts.

'I think I should dress, all the same.' The worshipful look in his eyes made her feel tremulous.

'Not yet, Teri, please,' Rafe said, taking a little box from his pocket, and opening it. Then, with his eyes never leaving hers in the mirror, he hung a pendant on a slim gold chain around her neck.

The pendant settled in the hollow between her breasts. It was lovely; a pretty green stone set in a delicate filigree of silver. But Teri was only conscious of Rafe's hands, warm and alive, circling the back of her throat.

'It's gorgeous,' she said unsteadily.

'I'm glad you like it.'

'What made you buy it?'

'I spotted it in a jeweller's window, and the moment I saw it I knew it was yours. Green and glowing. Beautiful, like your eyes.'

The blood had turned to fire in her veins, and beneath his hands her pulse was throbbing in her throat. 'I love it, Rafe. Thank you so much.'

'Seeing it around your neck is all the thanks I need,' he said gruffly.

'When did you get back?' she managed to ask.

'A few minutes ago. In fact, I saw Beatrix and Ed as I was driving in, and they said you were joining them for supper.'

'Does that mean you're coming, too?'

'Actually——' he smiled at her '—I said that I would escort you.'

It was becoming very hard to look at him in the mirror. 'Well,' she said, dropping her eyes, 'I really should go and get dressed in that case.'

'In a moment, Teri.'

And then he was pulling her up from the stool. Turning her in his arms, he drew her against him.

'I missed you,' he said raggedly.

'I missed you, too.' Her heart was in her voice, and she didn't care that perhaps she was saying too much.

'I couldn't help missing you, Teri. However much I resolve not to let my feelings rule me, I thought of you all the time.' She felt his lips move against her hair. 'I'd no idea I would miss you quite so much.'

Standing in the circle of his arms, with nothing more than her bra and panties on, Teri felt a tingling that was becoming familiar. Against her soft skin there was the exciting roughness of cord trousers and wool sweater, and even through Rafe's clothes she could feel the hard tautness of his body.

Sliding a hand beneath her hair, he cupped her throat, tilting back her head. Teri could not have resisted him even if she had wanted to. Their kisses were timeless, drugging, as if they could not get enough of each other, as if they needed very badly to make up for the time they had been apart.

There was not even a pause in their kissing as Rafe's free hand went to Teri's back and undid the clasp of her bra, then slipped it from her shoulders. They were still kissing as his hands cupped her breasts, caressing them, sending fire through all her veins.

Teri's eyes were closed, but she did not need to open them in order to see Rafe. There was not a part of that long, virile body that was not sharply etched in her mind. The taut legs and throat, the broad, tanned chest and shoulders. The thick eyelashes and the shape of his firm yet sensuous lips. At night she'd dreamed they were making love. And that was what she wanted to do now. She had not imagined that she could want it quite so much.

But now was not the time. Forcing herself to draw away, she looked up at him. 'Ed and Beatrix...'

'What about them?' he muttered thickly.

'They're waiting for us.'

'I'd forgotten,' he said, and from the feel of his body against hers she could tell that he was making a great effort to keep his passion within bounds. 'Oh, Teri, I want you so much.'

'Yes...'

His breathing was ragged as he released her. 'I don't want to let you go, but if I don't, I suppose Ed will come looking for us.'

'He might,' she said shakily.

'It's as well you said something.' Rafe pushed his hand unsteadily through his tumbled hair. 'You're so lovely. Another minute, kissing and holding you like this, and I might not have been able to stop.'

'I really must get dressed,' she said through stiff lips.

'Yes. Teri... Later tonight... may I see you again then?'

She was trembling. 'I'd like that very much.'

Teri spent the evening in a kind of happy glow. She could only play with the mountain of food that Ed insisted on heaping on her plate. Nor did she talk very much, but was content to listen to the others. Again and again her eyes would go to Rafe, his face stronger and more ruggedly attractive than ever in the dancing light of the fire.

Now and then their eyes would meet and hold, and Rafe would smile at her, and it seemed to Teri as if he tried to tell her something with his look. Then he would turn back to Ed, and respond to what the other man was saying.

Teri's quietness did nothing to detract from the lively conversation around the fire. Rafe told them a little about the things he had done, and Ed and Beatrix, who had had an entertaining week at Lelaanie, vied with each other in talking about what they had seen. The one thing the Moolmans did not mention was the gift shop. It was as if they understood that Teri wanted to tell Rafe about that herself, and she was grateful for their silence.

The fire had died low when Ed yawned. 'I think it's time for bed, Bea.'

'I think so, too.' She looked at Teri and Rafe with a smile. 'I hope you two won't mind if Ed and I call it a night?'

There was a chorus of goodnights, and then the Moolmans walked off into the darkness.

Rafe put an arm around Teri's shoulders. 'Am I still welcome?' he asked huskily.

'Yes, Rafe.'

Arms around each other, they began to walk in the direction of her rondavel. They were near the main building when she looked up at him.

'Let's just stop by the office first. There's something I want to show you.'

'Can't it wait until tomorrow?'

But, now that Rafe was back, Teri couldn't wait for him to see what she had accomplished. It would not take them long, and afterwards they would go back to her rondavel and make love.

'It's something I want you to see tonight.'

'What is it?'

'A surprise.'

'A surprise that can't wait till morning? Sounds interesting.' His arm tightened around her. 'All right, Teri, lead the way.'

The room beside the office was locked. Without a word, Teri took a key from her pocket, unlocked the door and switched on the light. Rafe's arm was still around her shoulders as they went inside.

'Well?' she asked, smiling up at him.

Abruptly dropping his arm, Rafe stepped away from her. It was very silent in the little room as he looked around him, his eyes going from the tables heaped with gift items to the hangings on the wall.

'What do you think?' Teri could not keep the excitement from her voice.

His back was to her, but now he spun round. Dismayed by the expression on his face, Teri took a step backwards.

'Rafe,' she whispered unsteadily, 'you do like it, don't you?'

'I hate it. How could you do this, Teri?' His face was a tight, cold mask of anger. 'How *could* you?'

CHAPTER EIGHT

'YOU'RE angry?' Teri whispered incredulously.

'You bet I'm angry!'

She felt a little ill. 'It's just a gift store.'

'I can see what it is.'

Tears were beginning to fill her throat. 'I was so sure you'd like it.'

'If you were so sure, then why did you wait until I was away from Lelaanie, till my back was turned, to do this.'

'You seem to think the timing of this was deliberate, too.'

'Wasn't it?' His voice was ice.

'Of course not! I didn't wait for you to turn your back—although it's true that I wanted it to be a surprise.'

The tears had reached her eyes now. Involuntarily, she dashed them away with the back of her hand.

'Don't start crying on me, Teri,' Rafe bit out harshly. 'Not that.'

'I have no intention of crying.'

He did not have to know that inside her she felt torn apart. The magical evening had evaporated in seconds, as if none of it had ever existed.

'Tomorrow you can take all this stuff back where it came from, Teri.'

'I will not!' Her tears gave way to sudden anger. 'Don't think you can give me orders, Rafe. We're partners, just in case you've forgotten.'

'I haven't forgotten a darn thing. Including how close I came to saying and doing some very stupid things tonight.'

Teri tried very hard to ignore the pain that stabbed at her with all the force of a physical blow.

'We're partners,' she repeated.

'Yes, we're partners,' Rafe agreed grimly.

'Whether you like it or not. And you've made it clear you don't like it. It's the reason you tried to buy me out.'

'I wanted to buy you out because I believed our partnership didn't have a chance of working. This——' he gestured contemptuously around the gift shop '——proves I was right.'

'Would you mind telling me why?'

'Our ways of looking at things are too different. Our priorities, our values. We've nothing at all in common, Teri.'

'That's not true,' she protested. 'We both love Lelaanie. Isn't that enough?'

'No, it isn't. We'll always be in conflict. Things will never work out between us.'

'They'll have to. Because I have no intention of budging. We'll always be partners, Rafe.'

'Maybe not.'

She decided to ignore that. 'You say our values are different. I'm not sure that's true. We both want only the best for Lelaanie.'

'We differ on what that means, Teri.'

'Perhaps,' she conceded after a moment. 'But a difference of opinion isn't necessarily a bad thing. It can add vigour to a place.'

He took a step towards her, closing the gap between them. Gripping her shoulders in his hands, he looked down at her from his great height.

'Lelaanie has problems, Teri. Great problems. Animals are dying because we can't get them all to water. We've put in windmills and waterholes, but we need a lot more. Tomorrow I'll be back at the drying dam with the men, and we'll rescue as many animals as we can. But I don't have enough men to help me. There could never be enough men. And we don't have enough time to do all we have to.'

Teri felt shaken, as much by his closeness as by his anger. 'I know all that. You're not telling me anything new,' she said quietly.

His hands dropped to his sides. 'In that case, why do you keep yourself busy with such nonsense?'

'It's not nonsense! Lelaanie is still a place where people come to enjoy themselves, Rafe.'

'They do enjoy themselves. They keep to the good parts, the green parts, and they see animals.'

'There's more to a game park than just animals. People look on their stay here as a holiday.'

'We offer them everything they want.'

'Do we, Rafe? I see too many empty rondavels. You've said yourself that we have a problem with occupancy.'

'That's something that will come right in time,' he said impatiently.

'Look...' She took a breath. 'I don't know very much about windmills and waterholes. I hope I'll learn. But in the meanwhile, I saw a gift store as something people would want. Something that will make Lelaanie that much more appealing.'

'You should have discussed it with me first.'

'Instead I tried to surprise you. Is that so bad?'

When he looked at her stonily, without answering, she went on, 'There's a *need* for a gift store. People want a place where they can buy postcards or a chocolate bar.

Beatrix said she and Ed would have to stop off somewhere to buy presents for their grandchildren, instead
of going straight home. That shouldn't be necessary.'

Picking up a T-shirt emblazoned with the Lelaanie
name in bright blue letters, Rafe creased it between his
fingers before tossing it impatiently aside.

'All this cheap, gaudy stuff. Do you think we never
talked of a gift shop? Your grandfather would never en-
tertain the idea of anything so commercial at Lelaanie.'

Teri made an effort to conceal her dismay. 'Things
have changed since Grandpa started the game park. It's
not fair to call all these things cheap and gaudy. Kids
will love these T-shirts. Look at the batiks, and the
pottery and the jewellery. All hand-crafted and lovely.'

Rafe stopped suddenly in front of the poster by the
door. 'What on earth is this, Teri? Pay for three days
at Lelaanie, and the fourth will be on the park. What
the hell is this supposed to mean?'

'If people book in for three days, they get the fourth
one free,' she explained.

'I understand the wording. I want to know the meaning
of this offer.'

'It's a promotion.'

'A promotion!'

'A way of drawing people, Rafe. People who might
never come here otherwise. We'll be able to boost our
occupancy rates.'

'A promotion,' he repeated.

'I've put up posters in travel agencies and a few shops
in town. People will see them, and they'll want to take
up our offer.'

'I don't believe it! I just don't believe it!'

'This is something I understand, Rafe. I've run very successful promotions. I know about advertising and marketing. This is the world I've come from.'

'I bet you have. But I never imagined you would stoop so low as to recreate that world here.'

For a moment, Teri froze at the steel in his voice. Then she lifted her head. 'Don't knock what I can do, Rafe. It may be very different from anything you know, but don't knock it, all the same.'

'None of it has any place at Lelaanie.'

'That's where you're wrong. It does have a place, and if you weren't so darned pig-headed you'd know that.'

'I know one thing,' Rafe said contemptuously. 'Your grandfather must be turning in his grave at the things you're doing.'

Teri looked at him steadily. 'He would not. I'm sure of that. My grandfather wanted me to have his share of Lelaanie. He must have known my ideas would be different from his, but he wanted me to have it anyway.'

'Stuart obviously thought you'd be serious about the game park.'

'I am serious.'

He looked down at her, a long, steady look. Teri had to force herself not to flinch from it.

At length Rafe said, 'There's obviously no point in continuing this discussion. It's getting us nowhere.'

'I quite agree,' she said, and watched him walk away.

In the doorway he turned back. 'Go back to America, Teri. It's where you belong.'

Her head was throbbing, and in her chest all she felt was a dull pain. But the look she threw him was firm, and her voice was steady.

'No way, Rafe. I'm staying. And don't bother to see me to my rondavel—I can find my own way.'

*   *   *

At dawn the next morning, Rafe and the men went out as usual to the drying dam. They went again the next day, and the day after that.

Until Stuart Masters' death there had normally been at least eight men in the group. Now there were seldom more than six. The two missing men were old-timers who had been glad to retire with the money Stuart had left them, and so far Rafe had not managed to replace them.

All day the sun beat fiercely down on Lelaanie and the surrounding countryside. Now and then the sky would cloud over, and Teri would spend the day anxiously wondering if it would rain. Occasionally there was even a slight drizzle, but it was never enough to make a difference to the parched veld and the drying rivers and waterholes. It was not surprising that the men returned to camp every night looking exhausted and grim.

There had been no contact between Rafe and Teri since the evening in the gift shop. Rafe had not asked Teri again to close up the shop. It was as if he'd made up his mind not to demean himself with a futile request. In fact, he did not talk to her about anything, and Teri did not know how to break the barrier that was like a stone wall between them. Sometimes she felt as if the continuing cold silence was eating at the very fabric of her being.

About a week after the argument, Teri happened to see the jeep driving in at dusk, and yet another man was missing.

Summoning her courage, she caught up with Rafe as he was about to open the door of his rondavel. 'Rafe...'

'Yes?' His voice was impersonal, as if they were two strangers meeting for the first time.

'I noticed John wasn't with you today.'

'No, he wasn't.'

'Has he left us, too?'

'Possibly. I'm not sure.'

'What will you do?'

'I don't know, Teri.'

His voice was so heavy with fatigue that her heart went out to him, but she kept her tone matter-of-fact. 'You can't go on like this.'

'I have to. I'm trying to get other men in to help.'

'Is there something I can do?' It was a question she had asked once before with no success, but she had to ask it again.

'You?' He gave a short hard laugh as his eyes went over her trim appearance in the fawn cords and a paler matching silk shirt she had bought the day before she left San Francisco. 'No, Teri. I can't think of a single thing that you could possibly do to help the situation.'

But, if that was what he thought, he would find out that he was wrong, for as Teri walked away she realised that there was in fact something that she could do.

When Rafe arrived at the jeep early next morning, he looked astonished to see Teri, clad in denim overalls, leaning against one of the doors.

He stopped short. 'What are you doing here?'

'I'm coming with you today.'

'No way.'

'A flattering response,' she said drily. 'But I'm coming all the same.'

He pushed a hand through hair that was still damp from his shower. Even in the dim light he looked extraordinarily attractive. 'Where we're going is not a sight for tourist eyes, Teri.'

'I'm not a tourist.'

'All the same, you're not coming with us.'

'Here comes Tim,' she said softly, as she saw the first of the men approaching. 'And the others are just behind him. Do you want them to see us arguing?'

'Of course not. Look, why don't you just forget this crazy notion of yours, Teri?'

'Because I don't intend to take no for an answer. And I'm pretty sure you don't want to lose face in front of the men by letting them see me win the argument.'

'So now you're resorting to blackmail.' He sounded exasperated.

She smiled sweetly. 'If that's what it takes.'

'It's going to be a tough day, Teri. Another real scorcher.'

'You're not frightening me.'

She stood quite still as his eyes went over her, lingering on her face for a few moments before descending along the length of her body.

His eyes came up to meet hers again, and unexpectedly he grinned. 'Where did you find the overalls? Do you know that you're swimming in them.'

The smile gave her hope. 'Does that mean you'll take me?'

'I don't seem to have any choice. I never have had very much choice where you're concerned, Teri.'

'Rafe...' Her heart was beating a little too fast suddenly.

'Get in the jeep, Teri. But I'm warning you, what you are going to see will not be pretty. And if you should get tired, there'll be nobody to take you back to camp.'

'I repeat,' she said firmly, 'you're not frightening me.'

It took them over an hour to get to the spot which once been a dam. It lay in the area of drought-created devastation which Teri had seen the first day she'd gone out driving with Rafe. Only this time they were driving even further into the stricken area, and once again Teri was intensely distressed at the sight of the drying veld.

The sun had almost risen by the time they reached their destination. As Rafe drew the jeep to a halt on the rocky shore of the dam, Teri drew in a breath of sheer horror.

There were animals everywhere. Some were digging frantically at the sand with their hooves, desperate to find a few drops of water where once there had been abundance. Others, deeper in the actual dam site, were stuck, unable to extricate themselves from the drying mud.

'It's a nightmare.' Stunned, she met Rafe's waiting eyes. 'It's an absolute nightmare.'

He nodded. His own eyes were sombre.

'I...I knew it would be very bad, Rafe, but I never imagined anything quite like this.'

'It would be hard to imagine.'

'How can you ever get to them all?'

'We do what we can.'

'You rescue the animals one by one...'

'We pull them free of the mud. And then we put them into cages in the truck.' He inclined his head in the direction of a big pick-up parked some distance away. 'And we transport them to new waterholes.'

'I thought I knew what you were doing, but I never realised the scope of it.'

'As I said—it's not a pretty sight.'

'You should have brought me here a long time ago, Rafe.'

His hand was on the door of the jeep. 'You'll have lots of time to see what it's like. It's going to be a long day, Teri.'

'If you can stand it, I can too.'

He stopped her as she was opening her own door. 'Where do you think you're going?'

'I'm coming with you.'

'Not a chance!'

'Why do you think I came, Rafe?'

'To watch,' he said slowly.

'To help. Didn't you know that?'

The long body beside her was suddenly taut. 'I won't let you do it.'

She gave him a hard look. 'Do you think all I'm capable of is running a promotion and a gift store? Is that it?'

'You're a girl...' For the first time, he looked uncertain.

'I'm a woman, Rafe.'

'Yes.' There was a sudden glint in the eyes that swept her face. 'You certainly are a woman.'

She tried very hard to ignore the sensation his look provoked inside her. Now was definitely not the time for it.

'I'm also your partner.'

'Teri...'

'And I happen to be every bit as serious about Lelaanie as you are.'

'Listen, Teri, I'm sorry if I said...'

'Save the apology,' she cut him short, though she would dearly have loved to hear it. 'You're short of workers, and you can do with an extra pair of hands. I came to help, and that's what I intend to do.'

The look he subjected her to was searching. 'It will be much tougher than you think.'

The look she shot him in return was provocative. 'If I can't handle it, I'll let you know.'

Rafe drew in his breath. 'All right, then. Let's get going.'

A kudu was the first animal Teri helped to rescue. Scrabbling furiously at the sand in a futile search for a few precious drops of water, it tried to struggle when the humans took hold of it. Not for long, though. It was too weak to keep up a fight.

Teri had had no idea quite how heavy a kudu could be. After it had been sedated, it took four people to carry it to the truck, where it would lie on a bed of straw until there were enough animals for the first transport.

Next in line was an impala. And then a young zebra, all long, kicking legs and swishing tail. The group worked in teams, two or three for the smaller animals. The whole group coming together for the larger ones.

By nine o'clock, with the sun fully risen and the heat already starting to become uncomfortable, the first truckload was ready for transport.

'We'll have some coffee first,' Rafe said.

The calves of Teri's legs were weak with fatigue, and her back was aching. 'Is that something you always do?'

'Did you think we'd make a special concession for you?' Rafe asked. But he was smiling.

'I'd hate very much to think so.'

'We all need the break.'

By the time Rafe had opened the door of the jeep and brought out a thermos and some styrofoam cups, the men were all making their way back from the mud. They took their coffee, but then they stood in a group a little way away, leaving Teri and Rafe to talk alone.

'You must be exhausted,' he said.

'A little tired,' Teri admitted.

'A little ... Hm.' He looked at her thoughtfully. 'Why don't you give it a break for the rest of the day, Teri?'

'Are you kidding? I came here to work.'

Rafe touched her cheek, very gently. 'You've proved your point, you know.'

She wanted so badly to put her hand over his, to keep the roughened palm on her cheek. But she just said, 'I'm not here to try and make a point, Rafe. I came here to help, for no other reason.'

There was the strangest look in his eyes. 'You are helping.'

Coffee finished, it was time for the transport to a recently created waterhole about half an hour away. As he drove, Rafe filled Teri in on all the things she wanted to know; what had gone into making the waterhole, the costs, the time, the effort involved, his plans for similar projects.

'There's so much I don't know,' she said, as Rafe drew the truck to a halt beside a large pool.

'You'll learn.' Incredibly, he was smiling again.

'After what we've come from, this water seems like a miracle.'

'In a sense, that's exactly what it is,' he said.

It took them a while to unload their cargo. A few of the animals made straight for the water. Others, still somewhat dazed, looked uncertainly around them. But they would drink eventually, Teri knew. And with any luck they would remain in the area after this.

The heat had become almost unbearable by the time the truck returned to the drying dam. Teri worked harder in the next hours than she had ever worked in her life. By midday, when they stopped for lunch, there was not a muscle in her body that did not ache.

'You're not eating,' Rafe said.

'I'm not very hungry.'

'Have something to drink at least. You can't let yourself get dehydrated.'

'OK.'

She took the glass of fruit juice he gave her, but it was almost too much of an effort to put it to her lips.

'You're exhausted,' Rafe said, very gently.

She managed a faint smile. 'You could say that I won't be sorry to see my bed tonight.'

'Why not stop now?'

She shook her head. 'No way.'

'You don't have to punish yourself like this.'

'It's punishment for everyone. This dreadful place.' Her eyes were bleak as she looked around her. 'There's so much to do here.'

'You won't be any good to anyone if you collapse, Teri.'

Somehow she found the strength to smile. 'I'm not the type to collapse, Rafe.'

'No, darling, I don't think you are,' he said softly.

Teri's heart did a little somersault at the endearment, but she did not comment on it. Probably it had no meaning at all. Still, the gentleness with which it had been said helped her to get through the remainder of the day.

The long afternoon came to an end at last. With the sun beginning to sink, Rafe called a halt to the day's labours, and Teri piled into the jeep with the men. They were all smiling at her, shy smiles some of them, all of them smiles that seemed to indicate approval. Teri was so tired that it was as much as she could do to smile back at them.

Ed was waiting for them when they got back to camp. Eager, wanting to relate how things had gone that day at Lelaanie.

Rafe was helping Teri out of the jeep. His arm went around her, holding her when her exhausted legs threatened to buckle beneath her.

'Later, Ed,' he said. 'I'm going to see Teri to her rondavel first.'

'I'm OK,' she protested. 'And I want to hear from Ed how things went.'

But Ed had also seen by now how tired she was, and he too said, 'Later...'

With Rafe's arm around her, she made it to her door.

'You can leave me now,' she said.

He did not answer. Keeping his arm around her, he walked her into the rondavel, where she sank into the nearest chair.

'You can really leave me now, Rafe.'

He looked down at her. 'You'll want a bath.'

'All I want is my bed.'

'A bath first, Teri. You'll feel a lot better afterwards.'

'You could be right. Hey, Rafe, where do you think you're going?'

He grinned at her from the bathroom door. 'To run the water for you.'

'I can do that.'

'And I'm going to stay with you while you bath.'

'That's quite unnecessary.' Despite her fatigue, she could feel the blood drumming suddenly in her ears.

'It won't be unnecessary if you happen to fall asleep in the water.'

'I'm not a baby, Rafe.'

'You certainly are not. You are a woman who performed a mammoth job today, darling.'

That word again. That wonderful word. *What did it mean?*

'Well, OK then...'

So tired was she that she could make no more than a token protest when Rafe insisted on helping her off with her clothes. She had dreamed of being undressed by him, but in all her fantasies she had been delicately perfumed and madly desirable. And now, here she was, tired and smelly and dirty beyond belief. As far from desirable as any person could be. So much for fantasies.

He must have spotted her bubble bath on the shelf, for the water was scented and foaming. Shyly she stepped away from him, to sink into the warm water.

'You can safely go now, Rafe,' she said.

He was leaning back against the door, watching her. 'I'm staying.'

She sank deeper into the water, luxuriating in the feel of it on her aching limbs.

'This is sheerest heaven.'

'Good.'

'I could soak in here for an hour and never get out.'

'Just as well I'm staying, in that case. You'd fall asleep and drown.'

'You have no faith in me,' she pretended to scold.

'On the contrary,' he said softly. 'I'm beginning to have enormous faith in you, Teri.'

Her pulses raced as she looked at him, so tall and strong, so very masculine. His day had been as long and as tiring as her own, but even through the dust that covered him he looked extraordinarily vital and attractive.

Much as Teri would have liked to remain forever in the water, she realised that to do so would not be fair to Rafe, who must be wanting his own bath. As she stepped out of the water, she saw him coming to her, a big towel held wide in his hands.

Beyond words now, she let him fold it around her. For a long moment his arms followed the path of the towel, folding themselves around her. She felt his lips in her damp hair, and the hardness of his arms and legs against her body.

Then he had stepped just a little away from her, and was drying her. And she let him do it.

At length, he lifted her in his arms and carried her to the bedroom. Still holding her, he drew back the covers, then slipped her beneath them. All done as easily as if she'd been no more than a child.

But there was nothing childlike in Teri's feelings as she looked up at him from the pillow. On a dry throat, she managed to say, 'Thanks.'

He looked down at her, his eyes hard to read. Then he said, 'Have a sleep before supper, Teri.'

'I'm not sure I'll be able to. It's only six o'clock, for heavens' sake.'

He laughed at that. 'I'll be back. The trick, I think, could be to wake you.'

She was, in fact, sleeping soundly when he walked through the door. But she woke up quickly.

'Rafe?' It was quite dark in the room now, but the tall figure by her bed could be only one person.

'How are you feeling?'

'Much better. I never knew until now quite how good a bed and a bath could be.'

He switched on a soft table-lamp. 'You earned your comforts today.'

'How long did I sleep?'

'About an hour.'

In that time he'd obviously bathed and changed his clothes. He was wearing black cords now, with a black sweater. Towering over her, he looked taller than ever, the dark clothes giving him a sensuously dangerous appearance.

'I've brought you something to eat, Teri.'

She smiled up at him. 'History repeating itself yet again?'

'Not quite, because we're not going to end up fighting this time.'

As he drew up a table beside her bed, she said, 'I really should put on some clothes.'

He laughed quietly. 'You don't have to do that. What I saw of you in the bathroom was enchanting.'

But he agreed to look away while she put on pyjamas. Then she sat up against the pillow.

Rafe had brought a bowl of hot soup which they ate with warm, buttered rolls. After that there was a lamb stew which Martha, the new cook, had prepared. It was delicious, but even after her sleep Teri was still too tired to eat very much of it.

'And now,' Rafe said, when she had pushed her plate aside, 'comes the best part.'

'You've brought dessert as well?'

'I'm going to treat you to a massage.'

'Good grief, Rafe! You don't really mean that?'

'Don't look so alarmed, Teri.' He was amused. 'You must be aching all over.'

'There are parts of me which may never move again,' she admitted.

'Which is why you'll lie quite still, while you see what I can do. Roll over on your stomach and relax.'

Relax? she wondered. But his hands were marvellous, moving over her back, her neck, the calves of her legs with a sensuous sureness. His touch was a kind of magic, bringing warmth and life to her exhausted body. There was strength in his movements, but an amazing gentleness too.

'How does it feel?' he asked after a while.

Her head was turned sideways on the pillow, her eyes were closed. 'Wonderful.'

'I'm enjoying it, too,' he said softly. 'Your skin is like silk beneath my fingers, Teri.'

'You really don't have to do this,' she said unsteadily.

'I want to.'

His hands stopped moving, and she felt his lips on her back, between her shoulders. The kiss was so unexpected that her body jerked.

'Rafe...' she got out.

He did not answer. He began to massage her again, and now it was an effort to lie still as the most extraordinary sensations started to flame through her.

At length, he turned her body in his hands.

'How do you feel?'

She lay on the bed and looked up at him. He was sitting beside her, so close to her that she could see the golden lights in his dark eyes.

'I'm a new woman.'

His eyes sparkled. 'I rather liked the old one.'

'Did you, Rafe? I thought most of the time you thoroughly *dis*liked me.'

'It was never dislike, Teri. Exasperation very often, but never dislike.'

'Who will you take with you to the dam tomorrow, Rafe? The old woman, or the new one?'

'Neither.'

She sat up with a start. 'Don't tell me you're not taking me.'

Quite gently, he pushed her back against the pillow. 'Actually, I do have something to tell you. We have a full crew again. Three new men are signing on.'

'That's wonderful!'

'It is. And it's all as a result of what you did today, Teri.'

'I don't understand.'

'You won the respect of the men today. They saw that you were a very brave woman who wasn't afraid of pitching in and doing hard physical labour. You know how fast news travels in the bush. I was just coming back here after my bath when Tim came to talk to me. He knows of three men who are keen to join us. They're experienced people, Teri, and they're eager to work at Lelaanie.'

She looked at him with glowing eyes. 'I'm so glad! That will make such a difference.'

Rafe moved a little closer beside her on the bed. Through his cords she could feel the hard muscularity of his thighs against her bare legs. His eyes were on her face, searching and thoughtful.

'You also earned *my* respect today.' There was an odd tenderness in his expression as well.

'Oh...' she murmured inadequately, touched as much by the tenderness as the unexpected compliment.

His eyes were holding hers now. 'I owe you an apology, Teri.'

She had begun to tremble, and this time she was unable to control it. 'An apology?'

'Yes, Teri. I was absolutely wrong when I said you weren't serious about Lelaanie. What you did today proved that you're every bit as serious about the place as your grandfather was. As I am, too.'

'Yes,' she whispered.

'I was so antagonistic towards you when you came back to Lelaanie. I'm so ashamed of that now.'

'Oh, Rafe...' She blinked back the tears that welled in her eyes. 'Rafe—I have to know. Do you still believe I came back when I did so that my grandfather would change his will?'

'No, I don't think you did.'

'And the timing of my return? How do you feel about that?'

After a long moment, he said honestly, 'That part still seems a bit of a coincidence.'

Disappointment showed in her face. 'Then nothing has changed. Nothing at all.'

'Everything has changed.' There was a caress in his voice as he caught one of her hands in his, and threaded her fingers between his own. 'I really meant what I said. You've earned my respect—in more ways than one.'

'Well, I guess it's something to know that at least you respect me,' she said unsteadily.

'I do a lot more than just respect you.' His voice was husky as he bent towards her, slid his arms beneath her back and gathered her to him.

He kissed her then. A long kiss. Infinitely tender. And then he released her. 'All I want to do is go on kissing you. Making love to you. But it wouldn't be right.'

Beyond words now, she could only look at him.

'After the day you just spent, what you need is your sleep.' He kissed her once more, tenderly again, then walked to the door. 'Sleep well, Teri.'

CHAPTER NINE

TERI wasn't quite sure at first what woke her. It was only gradually that she became aware of an unfamiliar sound against the roof and the windows of the rondavel, and an unfamiliar warmth in her bed.

For a few moments she lay still, her eyes closed, her drowsy mind struggling towards consciousness. And then suddenly the warmth in her bed became a body, and her eyes snapped open in astonishment.

'Hey!' She tried to sit up. She hadn't known till then that an arm was folded around her—an arm which pulled her firmly back down again.

'Where are you going?' asked a voice she heard in her dreams, and a man's warm breath caressed her cheeks.

'Rafe! What are you doing here?'

'Enjoying the feel of your delectable body.'

'You could have asked.' She tried to sound annoyed.

'You were dead to the world, and I didn't want to wake you.'

There was a thrilling kind of tension in every part of her body. 'How long have you been here?'

'Long enough to make me wonder why I didn't try to do this a long time ago.'

'You're crazy, Rafe.'

Lifting himself on one elbow, he bent over and kissed her. Her response was instinctive, her body arching towards his as her lips parted beneath the pressure of his mouth.

'Maybe we're both a little crazy,' he murmured, when they drew apart for breath.

'Maybe...'

'And maybe I'm wrong, but I get the feeling you want this too, Teri.'

'Remembering the way I've behaved from the beginning, you could hardly be wrong,' she ruefully.

His laugh was a warm exhalation of breath against her mouth. 'I do know that you're unique.'

'I'm going to take that as a compliment.'

'You can, because it is. This is bliss, Teri. Lying with you, holding you. I could stay here for hours—if you'd let me.'

'I'd let you, Rafe,' she murmured against his throat. And then, as reality surfaced, 'Rafe, your crew. The men must be waiting for you.'

'Not today. Listen, don't you hear it?'

'Rain!' She had heard the sound as she'd wakened, but then Rafe's presence in her bed had chased it from her mind. 'When did it start?'

'A few hours ago.'

'It's a miracle!'

'It is, isn't it?'

'There have been clouds on and off the past few days, and I kept hoping it would rain. But I've been wrong every time.'

'I was hoping, too.'

'Will it be enough?'

'There's no way of telling. Depends how long it goes on, and how widespread it is. But for today it's enough.'

'That's why you're not going to the dam?'

'The men are all exhausted. They very badly need some time off. And there will be enough water for the animals in that area—at least for today.'

'It's a miracle,' she said again.

He lay back, his arms going around her, drawing her to him. 'Let's enjoy our own miracle, Teri.'

His hand had gone beneath Teri's pyjamas, and now it brushed the length of her body: the silken skin of her inner thighs, the curve of her hip and the soft mound of her stomach. It went higher, to her breasts, cupping first one breast, then the other. His touch was tantalisingly tender, and all the more erotic for it, appealing to a primitive female need deep within her, so that the blood surged like fire through her veins, and in her loins there was an aching hunger.

With his fingers he caressed her nipples. Long, sensuous strokes at first, hardening as her nipples hardened, making her more and more aroused and excited. And all the time he was kissing her, deep, hungry kisses, and Teri was responding with an abandon that she had never imagined even in her dreams. While his hands were making love to her body, her hands in turn were going where they pleased. Sliding over his long, hard body, revelling in the play of muscles beneath her fingers. Rafe's tautening told its own tale of his response to her caresses, and that in itself was a delight.

'You are so beautiful,' he said at length.

'You are beautiful too, Rafe.'

More than anything, she wanted to tell him how much she loved him. But she could not risk it. She had not forgotten how he'd rejected her previously, and she knew she could not bear to be rejected again. More than that, she was still not sure that she had his complete trust and, without that, mutual love could never exist.

He drew her even closer against him, and then they were kissing once more. Deep, drugging kisses that threatened to push Teri over the brink of sanity with their sweetness.

After a while, Rafe said huskily, 'I'm not sure I'll be able to stop.'

Teri found her voice. 'Do we have to?'

'It's the very last thing I want. I just want to make love to you. All day and all night, without ever leaving this rondavel. But, Teri... Teri, my dearest, there's something I have to know.'

'*What?*'

'Are you a virgin?'

Her eyes met his. 'Yes, Rafe, I am.'

'There's never been anyone else?'

'Never.'

'I've misjudged you so badly, in so many ways,' he said raggedly. 'I don't know if you can forgive me.'

'I've forgiven you.'

'You're a generous woman. A warm, generous woman.'

He kissed her again, very tenderly, and all the while she was aware of a passion which he seemed to be making every effort to control. 'It would be so very easy to go all the way with you,' he groaned at length.

'I wouldn't stop you, Rafe,' she said unsteadily.

'You don't know what you do to me with those words. I want you so much, Teri.' He kissed each of her eyelids. 'But since this would be the first time for you, my dearest, I don't want there to be any regrets later.'

'There would be no regrets.' Emotion was beginning to close her throat.

He drew a little away from her, so that he could look at her. 'It's more than the fact that you are Stuart's granddaughter, though there's that, too. All I want is to make love to you, but I have to know that you're sure about this, Teri. We'll have all the time in the world for ourselves after that.'

Next day the sun came out again. Rafe took a drive out to the dam. There was water, he said when he returned, not enough to solve the long-term problem, but at least for a while he could afford to attend to some of the many tasks he'd had to neglect in recent weeks.

'Just as well, too,' he told Teri later. 'Alec Marlow wants to see me again in connection with the estate.'

'You have to go away?'

He traced a finger around her lips. 'Unfortunately. I'll only be away five or six days.'

'When are you planning on going?'

'Beginning of next week. Will you miss me, Teri?'

She danced him a teasing look. 'Conceited man. You know the answer to that, you just want to hear it.'

'You could be right.' His grin was wicked.

'You haven't said whether *you* will be missing *me*.'

'Ah!' The wicked look deepened. 'Did I hear someone say something about conceit?'

There was a new quality in their relationship which made it very easy to tease. Not quite a sureness, for Rafe had yet to say that he loved Teri. But there was a kind of permanence which was very nice in itself.

A day or two later, Teri answered the office phone.

'Teri, honey, is that you?'

'Good grief! Larry!'

He laughed. 'Why on earth do you sound so surprised? Weren't you expecting me to call?'

'I didn't know when exactly you would be arriving in Africa.' Realising that it had been some time since she'd given her former employer very much thought, she evaded the question. 'How are things going, Larry?'

'Great! We're shooting huge quantities of film. Magnificent stuff. This is an amazing place.'

'Yes, it is,' she said with pride.

'Say, Teri, I thought we'd come out and do some filming at that game park of yours.'

'I don't think that would be a very good idea,' she said in alarm.

'It would be great, honey. A private game park. That's something we don't have on our schedule.'

Teri's mind was working rapidly now. She could picture it all only too well. Rafe disliked Larry, sight unseen. How much more would he hate a film crew descending on tranquil Lelaanie? He would consider Larry's filming as just some more commercialism, even if its end product was for educational purposes.

'I'm sorry, Larry, but the answer has to be no.'

'Think about it, honey. We could make a point of filming the name of the place. It would be a great plug for Lelaanie. A free one at that.'

'I wish I could say yes, but I can't. Please, understand.'

His voice changed. 'You owe me one, Teri. Remember?'

Her hand tightened on the telephone. 'I do remember. But not this, Larry.'

'Why not?' She recognised the note of truculence. Though Larry was generally pleasant and good fun, there were times when he did not take easily to being thwarted.

'Rafe wouldn't like it.'

'You haven't asked him.'

'I don't have to. In any case, we're really busy right now,' she said quickly. 'This week is hectic.'

'Next week, then,' he persisted.

'Even worse. Rafe will be away till Friday, and I'll be taking care of things on my own. Don't push me on this, Larry. Please.'

There was a moment of silence. Then, in a slightly different tone, Larry said, 'Well—OK then.'

Teri's hand on the telephone relaxed. 'Thanks a lot for understanding.'

They did not talk for long after that, for the line had begun to crackle a bit, making conversation awkward.

Teri was just putting down the phone when Rafe walked into the office. It was the first time she had seen him that morning, for he had left camp before she was awake. For a moment he stood in the doorway, just looking at her, and as always she thrilled at the sight of him.

'Hello, Teri,' he said then, crossing the room to where she stood, and bending his head to kiss her.

'Hi, Rafe.' She smiled up at him. 'Busy morning?'

'Busyish. How about you? People phoning for accommodation this early in the day?'

Teri took a breath. 'That was Larry.'

'Oh?' His eyes were suddenly alert.

'He's in Africa now.'

'And he wants you to meet him?'

'Actually, he wanted to come here to Lelaanie.'

'Did you agree?'

'I said no.'

Cupping her face in both his big hands, Rafe bent and kissed her again. 'Have I told you this morning how beautiful you are?'

Her eyes sparkled up at him. 'Not that I recall.'

'Unforgivable neglect on my part.'

'Totally unforgivable,' she laughed. 'And is that why you're here, Rafe? To remedy the neglect?'

'Partly—because you *are* beautiful—and partly to talk about the gift shop. Do you have a moment?'

'Yes, of course.' Would she ever not have time for Rafe?

'I have an idea, Teri. I wonder if you'll like it.'

Together they went into the room next to the office. It had come a long way since the night Rafe had first seen it, for Teri had worked very hard on it.

With no help from anyone, she had built display stands for chocolates and postcards, and had applied a second coat of paint to the walls. Amanda Webster had sent another batch of crafts, and all the different gift items were even more appealingly set out than before.

Rafe looked around him. 'You've really done a lot with this place.'

'Thanks.' She was pleased and a little surprised. 'Now, what's this about an idea?'

He gestured towards the long wall opposite the door. 'I was thinking, perhaps you and I could do a mural.'

Teri took just a few seconds to think about it. When she looked up at Rafe, her eyes were radiant. 'What a wonderful idea.'

'I thought it would be something we could do together, Teri. In our spare time.'

'I *love* it.'

'Of course, I won't be able to do anything just yet. But once the weather changes I should have more time.'

'There's no hurry, Rafe,' Teri said joyfully. 'In the meanwhile, it will be something exciting to think about.'

'I'm not an artist, Teri.' Incredibly, he sounded a bit shy.

'Neither am I, and it doesn't matter. We'll muddle along together and we'll have loads of fun.' And then, shy herself now, 'It will be great to do something together, Rafe.'

He was looking down at her, his gaze resting on her sparkling eyes, on her lips that were slightly parted to show lovely teeth, and down to the softly curved figure. Something moved in his jaw as he took a step towards her. Then he seemed to restrain himself quite forcibly.

'What I really came back for was some breakfast, then I have to go out in the bush again.' His voice was rough.

'I'll make it for you.' She looked up at him. 'This idea of yours... Does it mean you've changed your mind about the gift store?'

'I can see how much people like it.'

'Sales have been brisk,' she said with pride.

'Which proves you were right. There really is a need for it, Teri.'

'I hoped you'd see it that way eventually,' she said, feeling very happy. 'How about the promotion?'

His eyes met hers. 'I don't like it.'

'You still think it's too commercial?'

'I'm afraid so.'

It didn't take Teri more than a few seconds to understand what she had to do. 'I can get the posters withdrawn.'

Rafe looked astonished. 'You're such a feisty girl. I never thought you'd give in.'

'It's not difficult to make the compromise,' she said, meaning it. 'Not after the one you've made for me.'

Putting his hands on her shoulders, Rafe looked down at her. In his eyes was an expression which made Teri hold her breath. 'I have a feeling this partnership will work out after all, Teri.'

'I wondered if I'd ever hear you say that,' she said unsteadily.

Once more Rafe held her face in his hands. 'Can you tell Beatrix Moolman that you and I will be spending the evening alone tonight?'

'I'm sure she won't mind.'

'Will you tell her, Teri?'

'Yes, I will.' Happiness made her blood race like liquid fire in her veins.

Rafe kissed her again, quite a passionate kiss this time. But after that he made himself step away from her.

'The men are waiting for me,' he said raggedly. 'If I don't get going now, I might not get back to work at all.'

Teri was in the impala's new outdoor enclosure when the van drove through the gates.

It was quite late in the afternoon, and already shadows were beginning to form on the sunny ground of the camp compound. Squinting into the glare of the setting sun, Teri could see only that the vehicle was an unfamiliar one. And that was strange, because she was not expecting any new guests at Lelaanie that day.

The one person it could not be was Rafe. He had been away for only two days, and besides, he had been driving his own car.

The doors of the van opened, and several men emerged. Even more puzzled, Teri watched them.

And then one figure detached himself from the others. For a moment he stood still, his head turning to all sides as he looked about him. His gaze seemed suddenly to fall on Teri, and he walked quickly in her direction.

It was at that moment that Teri recognised him. In a second she had vaulted over the fence of Annie's enclosure and was running towards him.

'Larry!'

'Teri, honey. Hi.'

His hands sought hers as she reached him. Then he was pulling her into his arms, and before she could stop him, he had planted a kiss on her lips.

'I can't believe you're here,' she said, as she extricated herself from his arms.

'This ain't no ghost you're seeing,' he teased. 'Say, honey, you look great. So tanned and sexy. Makes me realise what I've been missing all these months with you away.'

He reached for her again, but this time she was prepared and took a quick step backwards.

'This is a real surprise, Larry.'

'I figured it might be.'

'Why didn't you call?'

'I did call, remember?' He was laughing, but she noticed that his eyes were watchful.

'I told you not to come,' she said slowly.

'I decided to come anyway. What the heck, we're friends, it's really no big deal.'

She was struggling to maintain her composure. 'Who are all those men?'

'My crew.'

'You don't still plan on filming Lelaanie?'

'Sure do.'

'That's impossible, Larry.'

'Come on, honey, you're making too much of this,' he said indulgently.

'I wish you'd go, Larry.'

'Now?'

'It would be best.'

'It's getting dark, Teri. We wouldn't make it out of the park before nightfall.'

'You deliberately took a chance,' she said slowly. 'You knew that if you came in the late afternoon I wouldn't be able to turn you away.'

'What if I did?'

She was making a great effort to keep her temper in check. 'You cannot film Lelaanie.'

Before she could stop him, he had put his hand on her arm. 'I get the feeling there's something you've forgotten, Teri. You do still owe me one.'

'Yes, but...'

He did not let her finish the sentence. 'I didn't make a big thing about extending your leave when your grandfather wanted you to stay on here. I kept your job open.'

'I'm very grateful to you for all that,' she said unhappily. 'Really I am.'

'Then what's the problem? I'm not asking for anything very much, Teri. Just to shoot some film of this place.'

'Rafe would never allow it, Larry.'

'But Rafe isn't here,' he said with a smile.

'How do you know that?'

'You told me so yourself. Remember? Today is Tuesday, and Rafe isn't expected back until Friday.'

Until that moment she had forgotten telling him about Rafe's movements. 'Yes, I remember.'

She looked at him, and for the first time she was seeing a jawline that was a bit too weak, a smile that was a little too boyish. For sheer strength and masculinity, Larry could not even begin to compare with Rafe.

'You took advantage of a chance remark, Larry.'

'Maybe I did.'

'Rafe would hate this.'

'I'll be gone before he gets back, so he'll never know I was here. Not unless you choose to tell him.'

'I can't lie to him, Larry. If I didn't tell Rafe about this, it would be the same as telling a lie.'

He was looking at her, an odd expression in his eyes. At length he said, 'I can see there's not much point going on with this.'

She was relieved. 'There isn't.'

'But since it's getting too dark to leave here now, do you think you can spare us some beds for the night?'

'You're in luck there—we have two empty rondavels. And you must all have a braai with me.'

'A braai? You used to call it a barbecue.'

Teri smiled at that. 'When I first arrived at Lelaanie, Rafe complained I'd become too American. Now you're doing the same in reverse.'

'The braai was great, Teri.'

She laughed. 'See, Larry, you're saying it too.'

'Did I get the accent right?' He was laughing as well.

'Just about.'

He reached for her hand. 'Still mad at me, honey?'

The braai was long over, and Larry's crew, pleading tiredness after a long day, had retired to their rondavels. Even Beatrix and Ed Moolman, who had been intrigued by the Americans, had gone to bed. Only Teri and Larry were left sitting by the fire.

Gently Teri withdrew her hand from Larry's. 'You shouldn't have taken advantage of Rafe's absence.'

'Then you are still mad?'

She hesitated a moment. 'A little.'

'You really mean that?'

He sounded so boyishly disappointed that Teri gave up the fight. 'It's not easy to be mad at you, Larry. We've been friends too long for that. And it's true that you couldn't have been more understanding when I came here to Lelaanie.'

'I kept hoping you'd be back.'

'At first I really thought I would be. And then...well, my grandfather entrusted me with Lelaanie. It was the one thing I never expected.'

'I see...'

She looked at him across the fire. 'Tell me all the news of San Francisco.'

'That's my Teri! I was beginning to think you'd never ask. What shall I tell you first?'

'My mother and Philip. Do you ever see them?'

'Sometimes. They're both well, and send you their love.'

'Oh, Larry, thanks. Needless to say, mine goes back to them both. I so often wonder if my mother has got over the shock of my decision to stay here.'

'I think she's beginning to accept it. By the way, she asked me to bring her back some photos of you taken here at Lelaanie.'

'You were so sure you'd be seeing me, then?'

'I knew I was going to do my best.'

'And you did.'

But she wasn't angry this time. Larry shouldn't have taken advantage of Rafe's absence to come here. But Larry was Larry. Funny, easy-going in some things, stubbornly persistent in others. So different from Rafe that he would be genuinely at a loss to understand why Rafe would object to his presence at Lelaanie.

'What about work?' Teri asked. 'When I left you were just starting the school special about teenage circus acrobats.'

'We finished that, and it's been pretty well received.'

'Great! I know I'd have enjoyed helping you with that.'

'Instead I had to make do with Glenda.'

'Glenda?'

'Your temporary replacement.'

Teri was surprised. 'Temporary even now, when you know I won't be back?'

'I've lived in hope, Teri. Somehow I could never really picture you making your life in the wilds of Africa.'

'It's what I've done, Larry.'

'Lelaanie is really home, is it, Teri?'

Looking away from Larry, Teri's eyes moved in the direction of the fence. There was no moon, and the stars were covered by a blanket of cloud, making the night very dark. The air was alive with the sounds of the bushveld night: the incessant shrilling of the crickets, the scufflings of small animals. Then a strange high-pitched laugh came from somewhere nearby.

'A hyena,' she said.

'How do you know?'

She laughed softly. 'I know. I've always known, ever since I was a little girl. I love all the sounds, Larry. Night after night I sit here by the fire and listen to them. And the smells. Did you know the bushveld has a special smell of its own?'

'I think you've answered my first question,' he said quietly.

'I think I have, Larry.'

'Do you never miss America?'

'Often. How could I not? So many people I care about are there. My mother and Philip. You. My friends.' She leaned forward and spread her hands over the warm air rising from the fire. 'But Lelaanie is home now, Larry. Can you understand?'

'I'm trying to.'

'It's part of me. The bush, the animals. I loved Lelaanie when I was growing up. And when I returned, it didn't take me very long to know that I love it still. I guess there's more of my grandfather in me than I ever realised.'

'And where,' Larry asked, 'does Rafe fit into the picture?'

'He's my partner,' Teri said crisply.

'Business only?'

'*Larry!*'

'Forgive me, honey, but I can't help wondering. You never used to mind a bit of harmless flirtation, yet now you flinch any time I touch you. You don't want me filming Lelaanie because Rafe will object. So now I'm curious—does he have anything to do with your determination to stay here?'

'A little.'

'You're in love with him?'

'Yes,' she said honestly.

'Lucky guy to get my girl.'

'I was never your girl, Larry,' Teri said gently. 'You don't have room for just one girl in your life.'

'But if I did have, I'd have liked her to be you, Teri,' he said softly.

'Why, Larry...' She was touched.

'I hope Rafe realises how lucky he is that you're in love with him.'

'Actually, I've never told him.'

'Why not?' He sounded surprised.

'It's not something I can just tell him. I mean... I don't even know if he...' Abruptly she stopped. 'Look, it's really hard for me to talk about Rafe with you.'

To her relief, Larry was content to leave it at that. Quite easily, he turned the talk to other topics after that.

They talked for hours. Now and then Teri would put a new log on the fire, and they would watch the flames springing to life once more. There was so much to talk about.

It was almost midnight—an unheard of time in a place where people rose with the dawn—when they eventually decided to call it a night. Outside Teri's rondavel, Larry dropped a light kiss on her lips, but he did not try to press her for more.

'It's been great, honey,' was all he said, before walking off into the night.

Teri sat up with a start the next morning. The sun was already streaming through the windows, and the guests would have left Lelaanie hours ago with the guides. She could not remember the last time she had slept so long.

Larry! She remembered him suddenly. Larry and his film crew would be wanting to make an early start, for their next stop was the Kruger National Park, a drive of several hours from Lelaanie. They would be impatient to say goodbye to her.

Quickly she showered, dressed, and hurried out of her rondavel. She was making for the open area of the camp compound when she came to an abrupt stop.

Cameras whirred. While one cameraman was filming guests relaxing on Lelaanie's main veranda, another seemed to be focusing on Annie's enclosure. A man wearing headphones was consulting a clipboard, and someone else was busy doing something to electric wires. In the centre of all the activity was Larry. To Teri's practised eye, he was directing operations.

He did not see her advance on him. Only at her shocked 'Larry!' did he turn.

'Honey! Hi! Isn't it a great day?'

'Is it? I hadn't noticed.'

'Hey, Teri...'

'What's happening here? No, don't even bother to answer that. I can see perfectly well what's going on.'

'No need to get upset,' he begged.

'I thought I made it quite clear that you couldn't do any filming here.'

'What we're doing isn't so bad, Teri. Mainly, we're just getting some footage of this lovely setting. It's all so beautiful. You don't really mind, do you, honey?' There was a note of pleading in his voice.

'I told you, Rafe would hate it.'

'Lelaanie's name won't appear anywhere in the film, Teri.'

'It won't?' she asked doubtfully.

'Scout's honour. Any film we shoot here will be edited in with footage of other game parks. There will just be a few words about this being a private park. Our viewers will love it, Teri. The hill setting with the view over the river. The bougainvillaea climbing the walls of the rondavels, and the flame trees. And those funny blue birds jumping around the picnic tables looking for scraps.'

It was very hard to remain angry in the face of such reasonableness. 'You're quite sure Lelaanie's name won't be appearing?'

'No, dummy, it won't. Though why anyone would say no to a great free plug is beyond me.'

What could she say? Do? She could hardly demand that the cameramen surrender their film to her. The damage—if it was in fact damage—was already done. And, she had to admit, none of it seemed at all damaging.

'Well, OK,' she said at last.

'That's my girl. We'll be off after this, Teri. We don't want to be late getting to the Kruger National Park.'

'Yes.' Last night by the fire she had enjoyed his companionship, but now she would be glad to see him go.

'But before we leave we have to get some photos.'

'Photos?'

'The ones I promised to bring back for your mother and Philip.'

'I don't think I'm in the mood for photos, Larry.'

'Come on, Teri, think how disappointed your mother will be if I go back without them.'

Larry was an expert photographer. In no time at all he had taken several pictures. Teri leaning against the fence, looking across the river. Teri in front of her rondavel, against the backdrop of the purple bougainvillaea that climbed the whitewashed wall; and after that in various other pretty places in the compound.

'That's enough,' she protested at last.

'I must have at least one of us together. For old time's sake.' Larry called to one of his crew. 'Hey, Bill, can you spare a second? Come here and take a photo.'

They stood together by the fence, and Larry put his arm around Teri's shoulder.

'My special girl and me. Make it a good one, Bill,' he called.

'Do my best. Ready, you guys?'

Larry drew Teri a little closer. 'Ready as we'll ever be.'

'Say cheese,' ordered Bill.

But Bill's finger, about to press down on the camera, suddenly wavered. His expression, as he glanced sideways, was confused.

Teri's eyes followed the direction of his gaze. A moment later she felt her muscles tighten inside her.

Not five yards away from them was an advancing man. An obviously furious man, every inch of his face and body betokening danger.

'Rafe!' Teri whispered in horror.

'What the hell is going on here?' Rafe demanded.

It was Larry who spoke before Teri could get out another word. 'Rafe?' His tone was one of sheer dismay. 'Holy mackerel! Didn't you say Rafe would be out of the way until Friday, Teri?'

CHAPTER TEN

'SEEMS I spoiled everyone's fun by coming back early.'
There was ice in Rafe's voice.

It was a few seconds before Teri's paralysed vocal
cords were able to function again. 'Of course not.' The
words came out jerkily.

But Rafe appeared not to have heard her. Without
another word, without even another look, he strode
away.

'Holy mackerel!' Larry said again.

Teri ignored him. Her eyes were fixed on the taut lines
of Rafe's swiftly moving figure.

'Gee, Teri, I'm sorry,' Larry said. 'I didn't mean to
cause you any trouble. I guess I wasn't thinking clearly,
and the words just came out somehow. I wish I could
take them back.'

'I have to go after him.'

He tried to detain her as she made to walk away. 'Let
me come with you.'

'No.'

'I'll tell him what happened. That the whole thing is
my fault. That I took unfair advantage of a situation.'

'Thanks, Larry.' She had already taken a step away
from him. 'But this is something I have to do alone.'

'Well, if you're sure...'

'I am.'

'I'll tell the guys to start packing. We can be ready to
leave in half an hour.'

'Yes.'

'I'm really sorry things had to end this way, but it was great seeing you again, honey. And if you ever do decide to come back home, let me know. There'll always be a place for you at Anderson's.'

But Teri's mind was not on Larry and the job he insisted on keeping for her. 'I really do have to go and speak to Rafe.'

'I know. Listen, Teri, the guy may be feeling a little sore right now, but he'll understand the moment you explain.'

'I hope you're right.'

'Is this goodbye, Teri, or will I see you before we leave?'

She would not let Rafe intimidate her to the point where she had to be rude to her friends. 'You'll see me, Larry,' she said.

Outside Rafe's rondavel Teri hesitated just a moment. Then she knocked. At the harshness of his 'come in' she flinched. But her head was high and she was trying to smile as she opened the door and walked in.

She found him in the bedroom, unpacking. He did not bother to look up at her as she entered.

'Hello, Rafe.'

His only reply was a shrug, as he continued to take the clothes out of his case. The smile had left her face. Now it was an effort to breathe.

'Rafe, I'm sorry.'

Still no answer.

'Listen—I know how you feel about finding Larry here.'

For the first time he looked at her. Beneath his tan his face was very pale, and over his high cheekbones the skin was tight. Teri had seen Rafe angry, but never quite as angry as he was now.

'Do you know how I feel, Teri? Do you really?'

'Yes,' she said unsteadily, 'and I want to explain.'

She put her hand on his arm, and felt it become steel beneath her fingers. 'You see, Rafe...'

He lifted her fingers from his arm, as he interrupted her. 'There's just one thing I want to know from you, Teri. The day Larry phoned, did you tell him that I would be away, and for how long?'

'You don't understand.'

'Did you tell him that?'

'Yes, I did, but...'

'That's all I need to know.'

'Please, let me explain.'

'Explain what, exactly?' The eyes that met hers were filled with contempt. 'That I spoiled everything for you by returning to Lelaanie a few days early? That I would never have known about Larry's visit if I'd done the considerate thing and let you know in advance of my plans?'

Inside Teri, despair was being replaced by anger. 'You really don't want me to explain, do you, Rafe?'

'I'm in no mood to hear your excuses.'

She gave it one more try. 'Things aren't always what they seem, you know.'

'You told Larry precisely how long I would be away. When I would be back. That's as much as I need to know.'

Teri looked at Rafe, so hard, so angry, so utterly implacable, and now she was as angry as he was. All at once, it was no longer enough that she was in love with this man. All she knew was that Rafe did not trust her, that he had never trusted her, that however much she loved him—and however much he might be attracted to her on a purely physical level—they could never have a future together.

It took her less than a minute to make a decision.

'You can buy me out, Rafe.' Her voice was hard.

He looked startled. 'Say that again.'

'You heard me the first time. I've decided to let you have what you've wanted from the start. You may buy my half of Lelaanie.'

His eyes narrowed. 'I see.'

'Have Lelaanie appraised, Rafe. I'll fall in with whatever arrangements you want to make, provided they are reasonable, of course. I'll be awaiting your letter.'

'Letter, Teri?'

Her legs were weak, but she managed to look at him steadily. 'I've decided to go back to America.'

'This *is* a sudden decision.'

'It's one I should probably have made long ago. Until very recently you said our partnership could never work out, and you were right. Larry and his men are leaving for the Kruger Park, and I'm going to ask him to let me go with them. I'll send you my address when I get back to San Francisco. You can write to me there.'

Praying that her legs would not betray her until she had left his rondavel, she held out her hand. 'Goodbye, Rafe.'

'You're sure this is what you want?'

It was at least the fourth time that Larry had asked the question. He took his eyes off the road and glanced sideways at Teri.

Her face was ashen, and there were smudges beneath her eyes where she had dried away tears. 'Yes,' she said, 'I'm sure.'

'I'm really sorry about what happened. Look, I don't mind driving you back to Lelaanie if you decide to change your mind.'

Larry, contrite, was an unusual sight. Teri managed a faint smile. 'I won't change my mind.'

'You really meant what you said about going back to San Francisco when we're finished here?'

'Yes.' The word emerged painfully.

'I'm glad,' he said, but he sounded doubtful. 'I mean, just the thought of having my Teri back at Anderson's is enough to bring joy to my heart. It's just that...'

'You feel guilty, Larry, but you've no need to. Rafe always said our partnership would never work.'

'It was a mean trick, descending on you when I knew he'd be away.'

'It was mean,' she acknowledged. 'But if it hadn't been you, Larry, it would have been something else. There would always have been some reason for Rafe to distrust me. I think I've finally realised that now.'

They reached Shukuza, the Kruger National Park's huge main camp, just before dusk. Larry had telephoned ahead, and although the park was full he had been able to arrange accommodation for Teri. Covering the mouthpiece with his hand, he had asked her whether she minded sharing a room with another girl.

Through a haze of unhappiness, Teri shook her head at him. A night spent beneath a tree with lions roaring all around her would have been preferable to being at Lelaanie now that she knew Rafe was lost to her.

Compared with Lelaanie's little camp compound, Shukuza was enormous, a little like a miniature village. Hundreds of tourists bustled about its sprawling grounds. A few, armed with cameras and binoculars, stood looking over the river in search of game, while others crowded the big complex that housed the restaurant and the store. Everywhere there were children, running, playing, while their parents turned steaks on the fires.

Teri's head was throbbing as she sat with Larry and the rest of the film crew beside their own little fire. Larry insisted on filling her plate, but despite the fact that she noticed him watching her, his expression concerned, she was unable to eat a thing.

When she thought her head would burst with pain, she stood up. 'Sorry to be a party-pooper, but I think I'll have an early night.'

Larry was on his feet in an instant. When they were out of earshot of the others, he said, 'Are you OK, Teri?'

'Just very tired.'

'You're sure that's all?' His voice was warm with concern.

'Quite sure. Goodnight, Larry.'

'Goodnight, honey.'

Before she could stop him, he'd put his arm around her and kissed her on the lips. It was a light kiss, making no demands of any kind, yet instinctively she drew back.

Will there never be any other man than Rafe for me? she wondered despairingly, as she got ready for bed.

Sally, the girl she was sharing with, was not in the room. It would be a while before she came to bed, Teri guessed. And that was fortunate, for as she drew the sheet over her head she was able, for the first time that day, to give way unrestrained to the tears that had been choking her throat since the moment she had left Lelaanie and the man she loved so much.

'You're missing him, aren't you?'

Teri turned her head to look at Larry. 'Is it so obvious?'

'I've been watching you all morning, honey. Your mind hasn't been on our filming.'

'I'm sorry,' she said remorsefully. 'If I'm going to be working for you again, I really will have to stop moping.'

'Rafe is a fool,' Larry said, startling Teri with a vehemence she had never heard in him before.

'He's never been that,' she said after a moment.

'He is—if he lets you go so easily. You had a misunderstanding. People do, especially when they love each other. Doesn't mean it has to be permanent.'

All day they had been busy working. Once they had sat for more than an hour by the banks of the Sable River, waiting for a couple of giraffe to drink. The waiting in the hot car had seemed interminable, but the resulting film footage would make every minute of the ordeal worthwhile.

Back at camp, the crew had gone off for showers and cold beers. This was the first chance Teri and Larry had had to be alone together.

'We'll be leaving the Kruger Park in a few days, Teri,' Larry said now. 'If you want me to drive you back to Lelaanie, all you have to do is say the word. 'I'm even willing to take you back tomorrow if that's what you want.'

Go back to Lelaanie? Teri's heart beat in her throat. 'You made the same offer yesterday.'

'I'm offering again.'

There were tears in her eyes all at once. 'You're very generous, Larry.'

'Generous?' He laughed shortly. 'You're crazy if you think that. I want nothing more than to take you back to America with me. I'd like to woo you—is that the right word, Teri? See if we couldn't try to make a go of things together.'

'It wouldn't work,' she said on a sob.

'I know that. Because you're too much in love with someone else.'

'Silly, isn't it?'

'Silly is what you are if you decide not to fight.'

She looked at him, startled. 'Larry?'

'Rafe's temper may have cooled by now. Maybe he'd listen if you tried again to explain.'

'I shouldn't have to explain,' she said slowly.

'If you really love the man—and I wish you didn't—then don't stand on your pride, Teri.'

'I don't think I have very much pride left where Rafe is concerned,' she said wistfully.

'Does that mean you want to go back?'

She hesitated only a moment before giving her answer. 'Yes! I may be all kinds of a fool, but I do want to see him once more. There's a part of me that says I'll be wasting my time, that Rafe will be sarcastic and cold, and won't give me the time of day. And yet I know that if I go to America I'll never come back.'

'We'll go as soon as we finish here, Teri.'

Impulsively she touched his hand. 'You *are* generous, Larry.'

He put his other hand over hers. 'I know when I've been at fault, and it's time I made amends,' he said gruffly.

As it was, Larry did not drive Teri back to Lelaanie.

Later that same day, as Teri was returning to her room after an afternoon spent filming in the bush, she saw a man leaning against the door. A tall man, lean and tanned and muscular. There was only one person who looked quite like that.

Rafe! Her heart skipped a beat as she stopped still, thirty yards away from him.

And then he was coming towards her, his legs covering the distance between them in long, quick strides.

'Rafe!' Her voice cracked with disbelief as he folded her hands in his.

'Teri,' he said brokenly. 'My Teri.'

'I can't believe you're here.'

'All the way I just kept hoping I'd find you here. If you had left, I'd have searched every game park in Africa till I found you.'

She had the feeling that her heart was in her eyes as she looked at him, but at that moment she didn't care. 'Larry was going to drive me back to Lelaànie tomorrow.'

'Really?' He looked stunned.

'Really.'

'We have to talk,' he said urgently. 'Can we be alone in your room?'

'Yes.' She drew a key from the pocket of her jeans. 'My room-mate won't be along for a while.'

Rafe's arm was around her as they went into the room. He pushed the door closed behind them, then he drew her into his arms.

Her arms went round him too, and they kissed hungrily, as if they would never stop. But at length Rafe lifted his head.

'If we go on like this your room-mate will be back before we've had a chance to talk.'

'Would that be so bad?' she asked mischievously.

He sat down on a chair, and drew her on to his lap. 'Yes, Teri my darling, it would be bad, because there are things I have to say.'

My darling. Said in a tone that was as much a caress as his kisses.

'I had to come,' he said, 'because what we have is a once-in-a-lifetime thing. It's too precious to destroy with anger or pride.'

She looked at him through a haze of happiness, scarcely able to believe what she was hearing.

'You have to know, my darling, that the moment I got over my anger at seeing Larry and his wretched film crew, I realised what a fool I'd been. I should never have let you go.' His breath was warm on her cheek as he spoke.

'Do you know, Larry said something very similar. He didn't mean to cause any trouble, Rafe.'

'Hm,' he said thoughtfully.

'I tried to explain yesterday. You see, Larry...'

But Rafe put his hand over her lips, shutting off the words. 'Not now...'

'You'll never understand if you don't let me tell you about it.'

'I'll understand,' he said, with a gentleness that confused her.

'But Rafe...'

Again he silenced her. Then he said, 'Don't you want to know why I came back to Lelaanie a few days early?'

'You'd finished your business with Alec Marlow.'

'No, my darling, that wasn't it.'

She looked at him expectantly. 'It wasn't?'

'I realised how much I was missing you. I couldn't stand not having you with me.'

'Really?'

'Really, my dearest. That's one reason.'

'You mean there's something else?'

'Yes, Teri, there is. You see, I came across some papers belonging to your grandfather. Papers I'd never seen before.'

She wasn't sure why she was suddenly tense. 'What kind of papers?'

'Concerning your family, and your lives in San Francisco.'

'No!'

'It seems your father left you and your mother with very little when he died.' Rafe's voice was even more gentle now.

'Grandpa knew that?' Teri whispered. 'How did he know? Dad…and Mom afterwards… They tried so hard never to let him know how bad things were with us.'

'I don't know how he knew, but he did. And it mattered very much to him.'

'What do you mean?' she asked with sudden urgency.

'Your grandfather set up a fund, Teri. Every month he had a sum of money sent to you in America. Anonymously, I gather.'

'That was Grandpa?' Teri exclaimed. 'Every month the money would arrive. Always without a name. We thought it was sent by a friend of Dad's who felt sorry for us. My mother asked him about it more than once, and he always said it wasn't from him, but she never believed him.'

'Now you know.' Rafe was smiling.

'Why did he send it anonymously?'

'Perhaps because your grandfather feared that if your mother knew it came from him, she'd refuse it.'

'He was right,' Teri said slowly. 'However bad things were—and they were bad—Mom wouldn't have taken anything from him.'

'There's more, Teri. You know that when you came to Lelaanie and your grandfather saw how much you still loved it, he asked Alec Marlow to change his will. What you don't know is that even in his original will, he'd left you money. Quite a large amount of money. He was always determined that you would be cared for.'

'It's amazing. It's all so amazing. I still can't quite take it in.'

'I get the feeling, Teri, that you still don't understand why it was so important to me—*to me personally*—that I came back the moment I saw what was in those papers.'

She was puzzled. 'I don't.'

'As you know, I could never understand why you'd taken so long to come back to Lelaanie.'

'Yes...' She was beginning to understand.

'Heaven help me, Teri, but I didn't trust you. You know that.'

'You thought I'd planned to come when I knew Grandpa was ill, so that he'd leave me Lelaanie.'

'I'm ashamed of thinking it, but yes, I did. Even when I realised that I couldn't help loving you no matter what you did, that one thought always bothered me.'

He sat back, so that he could see her face. 'Now I know that it would have been almost impossible for you to come back earlier, however much you must have wanted to. It could only have been coincidence that you came when you did. You must have saved every penny you earned, Teri, and even then I don't know how you managed it.'

'Actually——' she smiled mischievously '—I won some money in a lottery.'

Rafe looked amazed. For a few moments he didn't speak. At last he said, 'Why didn't you tell me?'

'I wanted to so often. But I'd promised my mother that nobody would ever know.'

'*Why?*'

'For the same reason that she and I didn't come back to Lelaanie after my father died. Dad didn't want anyone to know the truth about our lives in America.'

'I see...'

'Mom is still fiercely loyal to Dad's memory. She wasn't happy about my coming to Africa, but when I insisted she asked me to give her that promise.'

'And yet you're telling me now.'

'There's no longer any reason not to. Not now, when you know how things really were with us.'

For a while after that there was silence between them. The only sound in the room was the hiss and fall of their mingled breathing.

At length Rafe said, 'If only I'd known.'

'There's nothing you could have done.'

'You're wrong about that,' he said roughly. 'I'd have come to you in San Francisco.'

'Why would you have done that?' she asked over a dry throat.

'Because I love you. I've always loved you, Teri. It tore my heart when you left Lelaanie the first time.'

'I didn't know,' she whispered.

'I couldn't tell you. You were so young, not quite seventeen, and I knew I couldn't say anything.'

'That first day—you said you didn't remember kissing me before we left.'

'I was lying. I remembered every moment of that kiss. You don't know how I had to restrain myself at the time, Teri. You were so very young, and I didn't want to frighten you.' And then he said, 'I wrote to you, a few times, but you never answered.'

Her head shot up. 'I never received any letters. I kept hoping...'

'Do you think that perhaps your parents decided to keep them from you?'

She thought about that. 'It's possible,' she said at length.

'They may have felt it was better for you to sever all ties with Lelaanie.'

'Yes... That would have been it. I wrote to you too, Rafe.'

'You did?'

'I remember giving the letters to my father to mail. I guess you never received them, either.'

'No, I didn't get them.' He was silent a moment. Then he said, 'After a while, I told myself you were never coming back. I tried to forget you.'

'You said you were engaged...'

'I met a girl. Janet. She worked in the Kruger Park. I was very fond of her, and we became engaged. But however much I tried not to think of you, you were always in my mind, Teri. Eventually I realised how unfair it would be if I married Janet, and we stopped seeing each other.'

'Oh, Rafe... And all this time I never knew.'

'At least you know now. I love you, Teri, my darling. I love you so much. You're part of me, you always have been.'

She nuzzled her lips against his throat. 'I love you too, Rafe. I can't remember a time when I didn't love you.'

'I want to take you home, darling.'

'Yes! But I'll have to find Larry and tell him.' She sat up. 'Larry!'

'What about him?'

'You still don't know why he came to Lelaanie.'

'I don't want to know, darling.'

She stared at him. 'But, Rafe, I haven't explained about the phone call.'

'I don't want you to explain.' He was smiling at her, but she saw that his eyes were serious. 'Don't you see, my darling? I've wasted far too much time with distrust. You couldn't tell me about the lottery, but I loved you, and I should have known you wouldn't stoop to scheming.'

'Yes, but with Larry...'

'I don't know why you told Larry I would be away. Somehow it came out, the reason why isn't important. I trust you, my Teri, and so I know that you didn't issue an invitation to Larry behind my back.'

She was trembling. 'You don't know how much this means to me. I thought you'd never trust me.'

A hand reached out to cup her chin, and he tilted her head just a little so that he could look into her eyes. 'I'll never stop trusting you after this. Or loving you. Will you marry me, my darling Teri?'

Happiness was a wild, wonderful thing inside her. 'Yes! Oh, yes, darling Rafe!'

'Let's phone your mother and Philip. I want them both to come out for the wedding.'

'They'll come, I know they will.'

'And Ed and Beatrix. If the Moolmans can't stay on at Lelaanie till then, we'll invite them back as our guests.'

'That would be wonderful.'

'But first I want to kiss you again. I just want to kiss you all day and all night and never stop.'

'I don't want you to stop,' she whispered, leaning towards him.

They were still kissing when Larry knocked on the door. Getting no answer, he opened the door and walked into the room. He looked at them for a moment, and when he realised that neither Teri nor Rafe saw him he walked quietly out again.

And, as he walked away, he was smiling.

Coming Next Month

#3055 INTENSE INVOLVEMENT Jenny Arden
Elise looks forward to a break from hospital routine on a new assignment in
the Loire valley as physiotherapist to Luc de Rozanieux. Then she meets Luc
and finds he's arrogant, short-tempered and extremely demanding. Extremely
disturbing, too....

#3056 NOW AND FOREVER Elizabeth Barnes
When Angus O'Neil lands his hot-air balloon in Mari Scott's meadow, he
breaks into her solitary life. Despite falling in love, they make no
commitments. And when Angus, overcoming his fears, proposes marriage—
Mari's problems keep her from saying yes!

#3057 HOME SAFE Kate Denton
The last thing Lee expects to find at her grandmother's house is a stranger
living there. And a maddeningly attractive one, at that. But Allen Hilliard has
a knack for turning Lee's expectations—and her life—upside down.

#3058 IMPULSIVE BUTTERFLY Kay Gregory
Jet Kellaway is tired of her years flitting from job to job—and the meager
existence it provides. Things certainly change when she goes to see Seth
Hagan of Hagan's Employment Agency and he decides to take her in hand!

#3059 COUNTRY BRIDE Debbie Macomber
Why wouldn't Luke Rivers believe Kate when she told him she hadn't *meant*
to propose to him? She was still in love with another man! But Luke didn't
believe that either....
(Sequel to *A Little Bit Country*, Harlequin Romance #3038)

#3060 MAN OF THE HOUSE Miriam MacGregor
Kay is quite happy with her very full, busy life until Rolf Warburton arrives to
disrupt everything and puts her future in question. And she can't understand
how she can be so attracted to him—a man she doesn't trust....

Available in June wherever paperback books are sold, or through
Harlequin Reader Service:

In the U.S.
901 Fuhrmann Blvd.
P.O. Box 1397
Buffalo, N.Y. 14240-1397

In Canada
P.O. Box 603
Fort Erie, Ontario
L2A 5X3

Have You Ever Wondered If You Could Write A Harlequin Novel?

Here's great news—Harlequin is offering a series of cassette tapes to help you do just that. Written by Harlequin editors, these tapes give practical advice on how to make your characters—and your story—come alive. There's a tape for each contemporary romance series Harlequin publishes.

Mail order only

All sales final

HARLEQUIN'S "BIG WIN"
SWEEPSTAKES RULES & REGULATIONS
NO PURCHASE NECESSARY TO ENTER OR RECEIVE A PRIZE

1. To enter and join the Reader Service, scratch off the metallic strips on all your BIG WIN tickets #1-#6. This will reveal the values for each sweepstakes entry number, the number of free book(s) you will receive, and your free bonus gift as part of our Reader Service. If you do not wish to take advantage of our Reader Service, but wish to enter the Sweepstakes only, scratch off the metallic strips on your BIG WIN tickets #1-#4. Return your entire sheet of tickets intact. Incomplete and/or inaccurate entries are ineligible for that section or sections of prizes. Not responsible for mutilated or unreadable entries or inadvertent printing errors. Mechanically reproduced entries are null and void.

2. Whether you take advantage of this offer or not, your Sweepstakes numbers will be compared against a list of winning numbers generated at random by the computer. In the event that all prizes are not claimed by March 31, 1992, a random drawing will be held from all qualified entries received from March 30, 1990 to March 31, 1992, to award all unclaimed prizes. All cash prizes (Grand to Sixth), will be mailed to the winners and are payable by cheque in U.S. funds. Seventh prize to be shipped to winners via third-class mail. These prizes are in addition to any free, surprise or mystery gifts that might be offered. Versions of this sweepstakes with different prizes of approximate equal value may appear in other mailings or at retail outlets by Torstar Corp. and its affiliates.

3. The following prizes are awarded in this sweepstakes: ★ Grand Prize (1) $1,000,000; First Prize (1) $25,000; Second Prize (1) $10,000; Third Prize (5) $5,000; Fourth Prize (10) $1,000; Fifth Prize (100) $250; Sixth Prize (2500) $10; ★ ★ Seventh Prize (6000) $12.95 ARV.

    ★ This Sweepstakes contains a Grand Prize offering of $1,000,000 annuity. Winner will receive $33,333.33 a year for 30 years without interest totalling $1,000,000.

    ★ ★ Seventh Prize: A fully illustrated hardcover book published by Torstar Corp. Approximate value of the book is $12.95.

    Entrants may cancel the Reader Service at any time without cost or obligation to buy (see details in center insert card).

4. This promotion is being conducted under the supervision of Marden-Kane, Inc., an independent judging organization. By entering this Sweepstakes, each entrant accepts and agrees to be bound by these rules and the decisions of the judges, which shall be final and binding. Odds of winning in the random drawing are dependent upon the total number of entries received. Taxes, if any, are the sole responsibility of the winners. Prizes are nontransferable. All entries must be received by no later than 12:00 NOON, on March 31, 1992. The drawing for all unclaimed sweepstakes prizes will take place May 30, 1992, at 12:00 NOON, at the offices of Marden-Kane, Inc., Lake Success, New York.

5. This offer is open to residents of the U.S., the United Kingdom, France and Canada, 18 years or older except employees and their immediate family members of Torstar Corp., its affiliates, subsidiaries, Marden-Kane, Inc., and all other agencies and persons connected with conducting this Sweepstakes. All Federal, State and local laws apply. Void wherever prohibited or restricted by law. Any litigation respecting the conduct and awarding of a prize in this publicity contest may be submitted to the Régie des loteries et courses du Québec.

6. Winners will be notified by mail and may be required to execute an affidavit of eligibility and release which must be returned within 14 days after notification or, an alternative winner will be selected. Canadian winners will be required to correctly answer an arithmetical skill-testing question administered by mail which must be returned within a limited time. Winners consent to the use of their names, photographs and/or likenesses for advertising and publicity in conjunction with this and similar promotions without additional compensation.

7. For a list of our major winners, send a stamped, self-addressed envelope to: WINNERS LIST c/o MARDEN-KANE, INC., P.O. BOX 701, SAYREVILLE, NJ 08871. Winners Lists will be fulfilled after the May 30, 1992 drawing date.

If Sweepstakes entry form is missing, please print your name and address on a 3" × 5" piece of plain paper and send to:

In the U.S.
Harlequin's "BIG WIN" Sweepstakes
901 Fuhrmann Blvd.
P.O. Box 1867
Buffalo, NY 14269-1867

In Canada
Harlequin's "BIG WIN" Sweepstakes
P.O. Box 609
Fort Erie, Ontario
L2A 5X3

LTY-H590

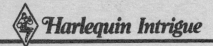

Harlequin Intrigue

Two exciting new stories each month.

Each title mixes a contemporary, sophisticated romance with the surprising twists and turns of a puzzler... romance with "something more."

Because romance can be quite an adventure.

Intrg-1

Romance, Suspense and Adventure